Nils, Globetrotter

Also by Hedvig Collin

WIND ISLAND

NILS, THE ISLAND BOY

THE GOOD-LUCK TREE

YOUNG HANS CHRISTIAN ANDERSEN

NILS, GLOBETROTTER

by HEDVIG COLLIN

NEW YORK ◆ The Viking Press ◆ PUBLISHERS

To my dear sister
Ida Andersen
in Denmark

Contents

1. Nils, the Island Boy, Is a Globetrotter   11
2. Nils Is Coming!   23
3. Nils Has Arrived!   32
4. Aunt Majel's Day   43
5. Christmas Eve   53
6. Christmas Day   72
7. "I Can Hear the Drums over the Mountains"   83
8. Bea's Birthday   92
9. Always Something Going On   104
10. Three Boys in a Rumble Seat   118
11. Good-by to New Mexico   144
12. Uncle Piper   161
13. Happy Birthday   176
14. Happy Ending   187

Nils, Globetrotter

1. Nils, the Island Boy, Is a Globetrotter

An island boy gets nervous when he cannot see any water. He is like a seagull. It is all very well to go a little way inland; but far from the coast he gets thirsty, he gets homesick. The people he meets have different ways. They do not know about wind or waves, about fish or boats.

Nils, the island boy, was sitting in the train his father, Mr. Hansen, had put him aboard in Chicago. His hands were damp with nervousness because he had never realized he would have to be so far from the sea. In Chicago he had seen Lake Michigan, but that was only a lake. It did not have the salty smell the sea does; it did not even look the same. It had been cold, though, and a storm had sent big waves splashing up over the promenade. There had been icicles on everything, and the light poles looked like ghosts. It was interesting, but it was too big. The houses were too big; the city was much too big. Nils was used to his little island in Denmark, and little towns like Svendborg and Odense.

Already it seemed to Nils that this long silver train had been rushing ahead forever, taking him farther and farther away from Mother and his little sister Bix and everybody he knew. It was even taking him farther away from his father, who had brought him to America on the big ship *Gripsholm*. But now Father, who was an engineer, had to go to work on a big dam and he could not take Nils with him. The dam was very high up, where there was no ocean to look at, only mountains, huge rocky ones bulging out of the earth. Just thinking about them made Nils very homesick for his own little island with the small hills where he could easily skim along on his bicycle, up and down, up and down, like a swallow.

No wonder Nils felt so lost. The Hansen family had never been separated like this before—Mother and Bix still in Denmark; Father on his way to the big dam; and Nils himself with a new address written on a card that he wore on a string round his neck: Mrs. Bea Johnson, Rancho Arroyo, Route 1, Sante Fe. He tucked the card in underneath his blouse because he did not want to look like a parcel.

Out of his knapsack he took a letter from his mother. He had already read it so often that the creases were getting worn, but he read every word of it again.

Holte, December 10

Dear little Nilseman,

It is sad to be left alone. Bix and I miss you, believe me. But we are as busy as bees and that helps a lot. We have so much snow, I had to have a man plow from the door to the road.

It will soon be Christmas, so I will send you my best love and a Christmas picture. I wonder what you will be doing Christmas Eve. Bix is making me something I must not see, and I am trying to get time to knit her some warm pants and stockings for our trip. I have made her a picture book, "A Visit to Santa Claus." I will show it to you when we come over.

I have to confess, Nils, I have sold your pony. It was good luck really, for I sold him to an old man and his wife who really love horses. They have no children. You should have seen the old woman, Nils, she was so happy to have the pony, and she promised that if you want to you can get him back someday. They have a big orchard full of fruit trees, a big garden, and a nice stable. You can be sure I looked at that barn before I sold them Spotted Tail; it is a nice, tight house, warm and cozy and full of hay. There is a little car that they use sometimes for a Sunday trip, to go to Mass, or to go haying in the field. So you can understand that Spotted Tail will have an easy life there. They are going to change his name from Spotted Tail to Ivan, the name their old horse was called. You don't mind, do you? Because he can always be Spotted Tail to you, even when he's Ivan to them. They have also taken Es, because the two animals were such friends and always slept together after you left. I hope you will agree with me that it was right to do this.

Bix and I can hardly wait to see you, but I still haven't got my papers for the trip—no permission to leave Denmark, no permission to get into the United States, and no ship yet. I am trying and trying, but it is difficult because I have to write on the papers which ship we sail on, and I don't have a ship.

I will write to Grandy in Malmö, asking him what to do. But I have also to sell our two houses first, or get a lawyer to do it, and then pack up our furniture that we will need when we have our new home over there.

How is it in America? Do you like it? I haven't had any letter yet, but I am sure one will arrive any day now. All good luck and kisses from Mother, who loves you. Also kisses from Bix.

Mother Ida

XXXXX BIX

Nils felt tears prickling against his eyelids, but he was not going to let them spill over. He was a big boy, going on ten years old, and he certainly would not cry in a train. Mother was right to sell Spotted Tail, of course, but it was hard to feel cheerful about it. That little Iceland pony had been his birthday present when he was nine. Nils had named the pony Spotted Tail from a book about American Indians—and now he was on his way to New Mexico, where there were real Indians. He wished his Spotted Tail and his dog, Es, could be with him to see them. But probably they would get terribly seasick if they ever had to take that long ocean voyage; Nils had felt green himself on the *Gripsholm*.

To keep himself from feeling too sad, Nils decided he

would answer Mother's letter now. He found some writing paper in his knapsack, and a kind porter set up a little table for him to use. Once Nils began writing, he forgot everything else for a while.

Dear Mother,

Where are you? What are you doing now? I miss you! It would be fun to rattle away in this train if you were with me to tell me about the things we pass. Just now we stop at a station, and through the window I can see real cowboys. They ride horses spotted like cows—really spotted and not with the spots painted on the way I fixed Spotted Tail to match his name. Do you remember that? And how you scolded me for painting Bix too?

These cowboys are long and thin, and their pants fit like gloves. They have silver on their belts, I think. Some of them even wear *two* belts, sitting far down on their hips—only they don't *have* any hips. It's a sight. I wish you were here to see them. Oh, why do we have to be in three places? I am sick in my stomach, maybe because the train goes too fast now that we have started again. I will try to be good and stand it because I know you want me to, and I know you are trying hard to get over here to us with Bix.

Poor Mother Ida, you are alone too. Come as soon as you can, and everything will be different. I have looked at the address where I am going to stay, but I do not know when I have to get off this train. There is a lady standing in the aisle, and I will try to ask her where I have to get off and the name of the town where I have to get a bus to Santa Fe. Father said Margaret from the *Gripsholm* may be at the station to meet me; but if she isn't there I should take the bus and she will be at the hotel in Santa Fe where the bus stops. I have the name of the hotel—La Fonda, Santa Fe—and the name of the house where I am going—Rancho Arroyo in Pojoaque. All the names are funny. Pojoaque is said "Pu-hu-a-ki." Now I had better ask the lady which station, because Pu-hu-a-ki is far away in a desert up between a lot of jagged mountains, maybe seven thousand feet up in the sky! I hope I remember the right English words when I speak to this lady. Wait a minute!

I asked. She says it is tomorrow at four P.M., which means four after noon. I don't know what the P.M. means yet exactly. I asked the lady and she said, "Post meridian." Excuse me again for a little while. I am coming back. The lady has invited me to have tea with her.

Here I am, back again. I was two long cars away, in one they call the Club Car. You would like it. You would like the lady too. Her name is Rannveig, and we had fun. She also is an island girl, from the Saga Island, Iceland.

You know Iceland. The people only live on the border because boiling mud and water spout out of the middle of the island and every mountain is lava or ice. There are no trees at all. And she likes it there!! The people live on sheep and fish, and the sun shines night and day the whole summer, but it is dark the whole winter. They have wonderful painters and authors who write about the old Vikings. She likes it—and she has red hair and green eyes and she smiles all the time. She said I should call her Rannveig because she said she knows you. Isn't that wonderful? But you do not know her, she said. She knows you from your drawings in the newspapers, and your books.

When she told me she knew you, I forgot and hugged her, I was so happy. Then I could feel my face get red, but she laughed and seemed glad. She made me forget being homesick. She loves Denmark as all the Icelanders do, because she said there is so much to be happy for in Denmark and so much sun. She is going to San Francisco, which is by the sea on the other side of America. She called it the Pacific Ocean—the one we call "the Big and Silent Sea." She says we don't know America until we have been out West. I am going west, so surely I will meet a lot of nice people. I am sorry I was so sad before I talked to Rannveig. Rannveig means "running wine" —did you know?—and she is just like running wine.

When I go to bed in this "roomette" Father got for me, Rannveig will be sleeping in the next one. Do you know what a roomette is like? It's a little room all your own when the door is closed, with a bed to pull down when the porter takes this table away, and a washing place and everything. Rannveig has come back now. Before I go to bed we are going to the dining car to eat together. Good-by, Mother

Ida, come soon. I put Rannveig's address in my book.

> Your son, Nils, Globetrotter

I can't see any water *yet*, but the sun is shining. I love you and send kisses to you and Bix.

The next afternoon Nils and Rannveig stood together by the window when the train slowed down at the station at Lamy. That was where Nils was to look for Margaret.

There she was! What luck! Rannveig here, and Margaret out there! Nils was soon going from hand to hand. The two girls did not know each other, but both of them knew Nils' mother, and they shook hands and talked a lot. Nils had only to *look* and leave all the talking to the girls. He held his cap in his hand, as a Danish boy always does, until he was sitting in Margaret's car. Then he suddenly realized what a lot he had seen.

"My trunk?" he asked and looked into Margaret's blue eyes. "Margaret, hello! How are you? Isn't it nice you could come and get me?"

Margaret smiled at him. "Hello, Nils, so you've finally come back to earth! I am fine, and your trunk is in the rumble seat."

"Oh," said Nils apologetically. "There was so much to

look at—the two Indians, you know. I never saw an Indian before. Are they real ones?"

"They are real, all right." Margaret laughed. "You will see a lot of them everywhere here. It is their reservation.

They are Navahos, very nice people and good silver-smiths. Look at that woman—silver everywhere on her blue velvet dress."

Nils looked and looked and looked! The car climbed higher and higher into the mountains.

2. Nils Is Coming!

"Does Mrs. Bea know I am coming?" Nils asked Margaret as they rolled along in the car. It was good to be with Margaret Nielsen again. He could speak Danish with her, and she made him think of his mother, with the same blue eyes and golden hair.

Margaret laughed. "You can be sure everybody at the Rancho Arroyo knows all about it now," she said, "but they didn't hear a word about your coming until yesterday. Such excitement there was!" As the car went on climbing, Margaret told Nils a great deal about the Rancho Arroyo and the people who lived there.

In Spanish a farm is a *rancho*. This rancho had three little houses under some big cottonwood trees; and all three were joined in a row down the hillside, keeping close together like three small children who are afraid of falling. There were stairs alongside leading from one to another. It was hard for Nils to believe that pretty houses could be made of mud, but Margaret told him it was so, and they had Indian-blue doors and window frames. And the window panes were painted with beautiful birds and flowers. The woman who lived there was Aunt Bea, and she had named her farm the Rancho Arroyo. *Arroyo* is another Spanish word; it means a river bed when there is no water in it.

Around this little rancho were three arroyos that could make life quite exciting sometimes. When they were dry they were good roads for cars. New Mexico has many such roads running along these dry river beds. Then comes a thunderstorm—a cloudburst in the mountains—and *whoosh!* The road is suddenly full of rushing water.

Those river beds are really something to talk about! The arroyo closest to the rancho was nearly always dry, but when the water did surge down into it from one particular canyon, it could drown a cow as easily as you could throw a stone. The other two naughty rivers spoiled everything they came close to—when they were there.

Just back of the rancho was a fence, and back of the fence the Indian land they called the Reservation. It was the Indian hunting ground, and the Indians' horses wandered round it. Downhill, near the quiet, dry arroyo, was a barn. The upper part was always open, so that it was full of birds, and the lower part was the home of Sarco, the horse, and Patches, the goat who gave milk for the boys to drink.

The two boys who lived with their Aunt Bea were certainly lively ones, Margaret told Nils. They were the sons of Mr. Garcia, the American engineer who had visited Nils' family in Denmark. Mr. Garcia was the man who had got Nils' father to come to America to build big dams. It was not until Aunt Bea had started out the previous afternoon to bring the two boys home from school that she heard anything about Nils.

Aunt Bea always went for the little boys in her car, which she kept on the top of the hill. The car was named "Old Pegasus," and it was nine years old, a good friend but sometimes cranky in its ways. But Aunt Bea was a clever woman. She knew exactly how Pegasus liked to be handled. A little roll down hill, and then *bang! br-br-br-pfut! pfut! pfut!* And Pegasus had started.

Down the arroyo Pegasus went. Aunt Bea had no way to walk or drive except in the river bed. There was no road at all. Nils could imagine what would happen if the water came. But it had not come yesterday, so Aunt Bea was safe and sound. In the mailbox that was down at the edge of the second arroyo, she had found both a telegram and a letter.

Quickly she read them both. She took her hat off and said, "Whew!" But she only "whewed" for a minute. Then the whole plan was made, and she and Pegasus went off to Nambe after the boys.

When Aunt Bea came back home from school, she read the telegram to the boys. It was from Chicago. It said:

TO MRS. BEA JOHNSON, RANCHO ARROYO, POJOAQUE, SANTA FE. NILS WILL ARRIVE AT LA FONDA IN SANTA FE DECEMBER 21 AT 5:30 P.M. SINCERELY, KRISTIAN HANSEN.

That was so surprising that neither Em, who was seven years old, nor Dwi, who was going on five, had one word to say for a minute. Aunt Bea could not remember when such a silence had occurred before. She read them next their father's letter, which ought to have reached her some time before the telegram.

Dear Bea, dear boys,
Now I am back from Denmark. It was a very fine trip. I made friends with a nice young man, Nils

Hansen. He is about ten years old. I would like to ask you, please, to be kind enough to take him at the rancho as a guest until his father comes back from working on a dam. Nils will arive at Lamy on December 21.

"That's tomorrow!" shrieked Em. "Bea, it's tomorrow!"

"I know," said Bea, and she went on reading the letter:

I am in Texas now and will not be back before spring. But I cannot imagine a better place for a boy than your ranch. Thank you, dear sister, I know he will be happy with you, and my boys will be good friends to him. He is a very nice fellow. Best regards,
Your brother, Maclovio Garcia

There was no silence this time.

"Bea, what is he like? Where will he sleep? Have you ever seen him?" It was Em asking questions that came as fast as hailstones on a roof. His blue eyes sparkled with impatience.

Little Dwi said, "What's his name, Bea?" His big velvet-brown eyes looked very solemn.

"Nils," Bea told him. "That's what the letter says, Nils Hansen."

"Shall we go to Santa Fe now? Can I go with you, Bea? When—how—who is going to get him, Bea?" asked Em.

"Now, boys, listen. You're the man of the rancho, Em, so I know you will help me."

"Yes, Bea." Em was tall for seven years, and he took being the man of the rancho seriously.

"Will you get the bed out of the storeroom? But *don't* smash all the other things in there. Calm down, Emerson, and do it slowly—"

"Yes, Bea," said Em. Out of the door he flew like the wind, and little fat Dwi trotted after him, like a smaller bird after a cuckoo. It was always that way with those two.

"*Emerson!*" Bea called out the door. "Em, come back here!"

Em answered from far away in the storeroom.

"Come here, Em! My goodness, that boy!" When Em came back, Bea said, "Em, quiet! You have to do your chores first. Give the animals food and water, and get wood for the kitchen, the fireplace, and the bedrooms. When you are through with that you can take the bed out. Do you understand?"

"Yes, Bea," said Em. He was a clever boy, as clever as if he had been much older, but he simply had to be awfully quick—just as quick as Dwi was slow. Em was always running, and after him came Dwi, calling, "Em, wait! Em, wait!"

The boys hurried down to the barn and gave Sarco and Patches their food. They carried kindling up to the four different stoves. After that they filled the woodboxes with lovely-smelling cedar wood. Then they disappeared into the storeroom.

They moved all the things out onto the floor—boxes, suitcases, coal sacks. Em crawled up on the big trunks. His feet went through one suitcase, and something went *crack* inside!

The bed came out, but all the stored things came out too. The boys tore out of the storeroom, leaving it a mess, and carried the bed into their own room.

There stood the bed at last, with clean sheets and a nice red Indian bedspread. All the toys were on the shelves. The room looked nice. But Lena, the helper, came in and turned the angel picture over Em's bed to face the wall. "An angel doesn't like to look at naughty boys," she said. Lena had worked the whole afternoon getting that storeroom in order.

As soon as she went out again, Em turned the picture around.

"Em," said Dwi, "don't!"

"I don't care," said Em. "The angel wants to see Nils."

The telephone rang. It was Margaret.

"Margaret, listen," said Bea, "a little Danish boy is coming!"

"I know," said Margaret, laughing. "I met him aboard the *Gripsholm* coming over. I will get him in Lamy tomorrow and bring him out to you."

And that was how Margaret heard all about the excitement at the Rancho Arroyo and could tell Nils about it. Nils thought it was nice they all sounded so happy that he was coming. But it was a very long drive they were taking to get there, and he was getting tireder and tireder.

3. Nils Has Arrived!

All day the two little boys at the Rancho Arroyo had talked about nothing but Nils. When at last they had to go to bed, he still had not arrived. But when they woke up in the morning, there was an angel like the one in the picture—and the angel was sleeping in the new bed.

"Look!" said Dwi. "Do you think that *is* Nils? Just like the angel! Look at the golden hair. Do you think **it** really is Nils?"

"Crazy nut!" scoffed his brother. "An angel! Sure, **it's** Nils. Wake up, Nils!"

"Em, don't!" whispered Dwi.

Nils was most awfully sleepy. He had not got to bed until midnight, and after all that rattling about in the train and the car he just could not wake up. Em kept on calling, but it was no use. Nils' eyes were still shut. He turned over, scratched at his yellow silk mop of hair so that it stood out in all directions, and fell sound asleep again.

"Well," said Dwi, "he doesn't look like an angel any more. I guess it really is Nils."

They got up and went out to do their chores. Nils slept until ten o'clock.

The two boys had been in every other minute to see if he showed any signs of coming back to life, and they were the first thing he saw.

"Hey, Nils!" said Em. "We've been up four hours already. And we've watered our horse and all."

Quite suddenly Nils sat up in bed. "Where am I?" he asked, bewildered. He looked like a haystack after a storm, with a big question mark on top.

"You are here," said Dwi with his funny little chuckle.

"Here?" asked Nils. It was lucky that Lena came into the room just then. He might have been a long time finding out where he was from the two boys.

"Lena!" said Dwi. "He talks very funny."

"He doesn't even know us." Em was grinning.

Nils was really waking up as Lena sat down on the bed and smiled at him.

"Good morning, Nils. Did you sleep well?" Her voice was kind.

"Oh, yes!" answered Nils.

"Now, Nils, I will tell you where you are."

"I know!" said Nils. "I was just funny in my head at first."

"This is Emerson," said Lena, "and this is Dwight." The boys all shook hands.

"Who turned that angel around?" asked Lena with a little twinkle in her eye.

"I thought the angel would like to see Nils," said Em, and Lena looked quickly in another direction.

"Now, Nils, you just wait a minute and I will bring your breakfast," Lena said. "Then you can come up to the bath. Em will show you the way."

"Where is my suitcase?" asked Nils, and Em disappeared to get it from the main house.

He was back in half a minute and met Lena in the doorway with a big tray of breakfast for Nils. *Breakfast in bed!* The Garcia boys had never heard of such a thing except when they were sick.

Nils dug down in his suitcase. Mother had packed gifts for the boys and for Bea, when she had heard about them from Mr. Garcia, but she had not known about Lena. Nils was very embarrassed.

"Do not worry about it, Nils," Lena said. "If you are just a good man on the farm, that's enough for me."

Em and Dwi had a grand time that day, showing Nils everything on the little farm. They let him get into the piano box that they used for everything—playhouse, workshop, and place to take sunbaths in winter, because it had sides to keep the wind off them. They let him take a swing in the automobile tire fastened by a long rope to the huge cottonwood tree.

Nils was introduced to Silver, a dog with a very long nose and a curly tail, and he heard about the time Silver had had a fight with a skunk and couldn't come into the house for a whole week. He met Trusty, the tomcat, who was shiny black with a white face and stomach and white shoes. Trusty looked very sleek and was interested only in two bluejays, but Nils heard how sometimes he got into fights too, and would come home all dirty and with split ears. After a night like that, Trusty always plumped himself into the softest and best chair, where there was a good warm Mexican rug, and then slept all day. Trusty ate the birds in the trees, and the birds' children too, but still the boys loved the imp.

Nils went to make friends with Sarco the horse and Patches the goat. He gave each of them a carrot.

"Ma-a-a!" said Patches, and she chomped her carrot. She and Nils were friends.

Sarco said "Hnnn! Hnnn! Hnnn!" in his nose, which was his thank-you to Nils.

Next to the barn on one side was a field of alfalfa that smelled delicious, and on the other side was a gateway over a cattle-guard. This was a big ditch with a grill over it, so that cars could get across it but the many cows and horses that ran round loose in the hills could not. But you couldn't keep the animals away when they smelled the alfalfa, and they were forever jumping over the fence that ran round the farm.

The boys brought Sarco out of the barn and led him through the little gate. To show off for Nils, both Em and Dwi got onto Sarco's back, and they were a fine sight. They met some Indian boys on horseback and shouted "Hi!" to them.

Then they heard the pound of galloping hoofs. A whole herd of wild horses were coming over the hills at a rattling pace. Em and Dwi made Sarco gallop too, but suddenly he had had quite enough. He stopped so abruptly that he tossed both boys off into the arroyo. Then he snuffled at them. They weren't hurt, so he trotted off back home.

Em was very much ashamed of having fallen off his horse in front of Nils. But Nils hadn't even noticed. He

had eyes for nothing but those wild horses. What a sight they were for a Danish boy! An Indian on horseback was galloping after the herd.

"That's Suapin," Em told Nils. "He has to get the horses back to the Indian land."

The three boys watched the young Indian rounding up the horses. The string of animals had to be rushed through the gate into the Indian Reservation. The horses knew that, but they knew some tricks as well. First they ran up the hill. Suapin took the shortest way, his horse springing up the hillside almost straight into the air. Sand and stones flew under its hoofs. He stopped. The other horses turned round, rearing on their hind legs.

Then the whole herd raced down again. The Indian boy gave his horse a kick, and off they flew to get in front again. Suapin whirled his horse round like a top, with the gravel flying up round him. The wild horses were together and took the path to the gate—all but one. Suapin used his lasso and got the outsider with a snap. The trapped horse dropped to his knees, with Suapin right behind him. The Indian loosened his lasso, and the tricky horse went rushing after the others through the gate. Quick as a flash, Suapin had dropped off his horse and shut the gate.

Nils was shaking from excitement, and his heart was pounding inside his sweater. For the other boys it was an everyday happening. They asked Nils if he wanted to ride home.

Nils did want to, but then they realized that Sarco had already gone home.

With great big appetites, all three boys went home to find an even bigger dinner waiting for them on a long red table. Em and Dwi forgot all about not talking with their mouths full, and they told Nils Indian stories during the meal.

Right away Nils liked everything about the Rancho Arroyo. He decided that he wanted to learn Spanish. All the Indians understood Spanish, and so did Hilario, the man of all trades, who came to help Aunt Bea when anything went wrong. He was a nice man who looked like an Englishman because he wore a white sun helmet, but he was Spanish.

Nils liked the little mud farmhouse on top of the hill. Under the big cottonwood trees stood the main house, with the hall, two bedrooms, bathroom, and living room. Next came a little house with only the kitchen. At the lower end was the boys' house, bringing up the rear like the caboose at the end of a freight train. It had three doors and three rooms—one room for Lena, one for the boys, and the storeroom, which Lena had already put straight again.

Everything about the house was so pretty! The doors were a lovely Indian blue, and on the one glass door was painted a gay Spanish rooster. The living room was beautiful, with a fireplace and adobe chimney and a big black cross against the chimney. There was only one arm chair with an Indian rug—and there was Trusty in it, looking very sleek and handsome against the blue. There was one wooden chair and there were small red stools for the boys. Like the walls, the floor was of the mud they called *adobe*, but on the floor was a big Indian rug with a blue pattern. The very long red table stood underneath the blue window with a wide view of the black mesa.

That table! It was long enough for lots of guests, and narrow enough so that they could reach everything. There was always something beautiful on it—flowers, or fruit, or candles, or a lot of food, or something more unusual. The boys could read at the table, and they could draw and paint there or play Lotto or Chinese checkers. Around the table stood eight Mexican chairs with all sorts of flowers painted on them.

From the table the boys could see out into the kitchen, which was the next little house. And it was a kitchen worth seeing, with cupboards painted red and blue inside, filled with plates with houses and flowers and birds on them. It was a real fairy-tale kitchen. And over the stove Bea had a long niche that held two rows of spices that Nils had never heard of before.

When they went out to play after dinner, Nils decided the Rancho Arroyo was just as colorful outside as inside. The mountains were purple and blue and red and green, and far away he could see the black mesa, the Indians' holy mountain.

Then a wind sprang up and brought a thunderstorm. Sand blew into the boys' eyes. The sun grew red and the sky got dark; the trees turned a pale gray, nearly white, against the raven-blue sky.

The boys ran as fast as they could up the hill. By the time they got home to the red table and Bea and Lena, the sudden storm had already passed. There was a double rainbow—two great arcs of colors, one inside the other. There were always some surprises when there was a thunderstorm, the boys told Nils—sometimes he would see *three* rainbows at once!

4. Aunt Majel's Day

*Tut-tut-tut-*TUT! There was an automobile coming up the arroyo. The boys jumped to the window to see.

"It's Aunt Majel's car!" they shouted to Nils. "This will be fun." They ran outdoors to meet her.

Aunt Majel was coming to teach the boys how to make tinwork for their Christmas tree. She shouted greetings to everybody and laughed just as much as the boys did.

She was a real beauty. Her hair was short and black and curly, and she never wore a hat. She was dressed in a white blouse and blue denim slacks. She looked like a tinsmith, and she was one. But Aunt Majel could do many other things besides—everything! She could paint beautiful Santos—little figures of the saints. She could write stories. She could *tell* stories. And how she could laugh!

Her car was loaded with exciting things. First of all, there was a huge beefsteak—and an enormous cake. Then there were three blocks for hammering tin, and a whole sackful of tools. The boys carried things into the house. They carried, too, an atmosphere of fiesta.

When Majel came, Em and Dwi knew there would be six candles on the red table for dinner, to make it a real party. There was always a strong, good smell coming from the kitchen, and Majel was out there talking over with Bea how best to do the cooking—onions, lots of onions, and garlic and chili, and *this* and *that!* And laughter always got into the dinner, too, along with the cheerful clatter and rattle of pots and pans.

"How are you?" Majel asked the three boys, and Nils could not help feeling he had known her almost as long as Em and Dwi had, which was all their lives.

"We are fine, Majel!" they all told her with sparkling eyes. "What is inside that package?" they asked.

"Oh, maybe something nice. Let's look." Out she took —imagine!—three packages of cigars, one for each of the boys, with three cigars in each package.

Em and Dwi looked at the cigars. They looked at Majel. They looked at Bea. And each look was like a question mark: ? ? ? Then Nils laughed suddenly. He had seen such things before.

Majel sat down in Trusty's big blue chair, giving the cat a push to make room. With anybody else, Trusty might have got down and walked off in a huff, but he liked Majel, just as everybody else did.

"Go on, smoke!" Majel said.

"You can smoke," said Bea, "when Majel tells you to."

The boys pulled the cellophane off their cigars, and a most lovely smell reached their noses. "Oh, chocolate!" they said. "Tell us a story while we smoke, Majel!"

So Majel told them a story about being taken to a circus when she was four years old. Then Em and Dwi told her about a circus they had seen in a big tent just outside of Santa Fe. Em had liked the seals best of all. "They could do everything," he said, "even talk and count and play the trumpet, and play baseball—nearly."

The boys talked and talked about circuses. Nils told them about the one he had seen in Denmark, and how he had put on a circus of his own after that. His pony Spotted Tail and his dog Es had done lots of tricks. Nils had been ringmaster, and his mother had dressed up as a clown and his father as Uncle Sam. "That was because we had an American visitor there to see the circus," Nils said. "Can you guess who it was?"

"The President?" asked Dwi.

"No!" Nils laughed. "Mr. Garcia."

"Our Daddy?" The eyes of both boys grew round as they thought what a strange and wonderful thing it was that their own father had seen Nils' circus away across the ocean in Denmark.

Majel was in the kitchen again, frying chili and garlic. The stove was going full speed. Pretty soon she left the rest for Bea to do and came back.

"Hi, boys, get to work now!" she said.

The red table was cleaned off, the big fruit platter moved away, and tin and a lot of tools were laid out on papers. There were three heavy blocks of wood on the floor, and beside each was one of the boys' own red stools.

Majel told them, "Now I will cut out a fish to hang in

the branches of the Christmas tree. That's for Nils because you come from the sea. You are the biggest, too,
Nils, and you can work alone. Here is a screw—the end
can be used for punching eyes. Watch this, boys!" And
Majel showed them how. "One bang with the hammer
on the screw—that makes a ring. Then you turn your
fish and give him a point in the middle of the eye. Always work on both sides of the tin. Then the fins—three
bangs with the hammer on the screwdriver from one side,
and three from the other side in between. There—isn't
he fine? Now, Nils, you work like that and give him
scales and anything you can think of to make him look
nice. Put lines on each side of the mouth from both
sides. You only get three tools—a screw, a nail, and a
screwdriver. Oh, yes, you can have this half-circle tool."

Then it was Em's turn. "Here, I will start you on a
pelican." He got the same instructions as Nils—there a
piece of tin, there a tool for the feathers, there a nail
for the eye.

For Dwi, Majel cut out a Santa Claus. What a noise there was while they all three hammered! And nobody—almost—hammered his fingers.

Bea came in from the kitchen. "Oh, Majel, may I do it too?" she asked.

"Yes, of course you may. Draw a big circle and cut it out, Bea, and I will show you how to make a nice dish."

Nils had finished his fish by the time Bea had cut out her big circle. Now all four of them watched Majel, the master tinsmith. First she made five circles with a compass. Then she hammered a design with all sorts of funny tools, first on one side, then after turning it, from the other side. It was going to be a most beautiful pattern, a whole big flower in the middle and a border of flowers out at the edge. The boys looked on without saying a word. They could not have been heard anyhow, because of the noise of the hammering.

"There," said Majel at last. "It looks nice, eh?" She took a pair of pliers and turned the edge up, bending it in and out like waves, and the dish was finished. Then she scrubbed it with soap and ashes until it looked just like pewter.

"You like it?" she asked Bea.

"Oh, yes!" Bea cried.

"A souvenir!" Majel said. "A Christmas present!" Oh, how pleased Bea was!

"Now let me see your work, boys," Majel said. "Perfectly grand!" she told Nils. "Yes," she said to Em, "not so bad. Better next time." Then she looked at little fat Dwi's. His Christmas Santa Claus had flowers on his face and stars and points everywhere. Majel gave him a few more little trimmings, and he was a very funny and most original Santa Claus. "Now you make a hole!" Majel said. "So! That's right."

"Ouch!" said Dwi. He had made two holes, one of them in his own forehead. His head had been too close to the hammer.

Majel laughed, so Dwi did too. "That's a big boy!"

Majel said. "We all get some bangs in this work. Now you can put a string through the hole in your Santa Claus and hang him on the Christmas tree. Tonight I shall teach Bea how to solder, and she can teach you when she has time."

It was time to bring the beefsteak to the table now. The red table was whisked clear of bits of tin and paper and tools and laid out for a party dinner. There were candles, fruit, glasses, milk, wine, flowers, and plates of all colors with flowers painted everywhere on them. Big smiles and hungry stomachs completed the scene.

The boys had another story before they went to bed. They were all still sitting round the table, Majel and Bea with their coffee and cigarettes, the boys puffing away at their chocolate cigars, but not bothering to nibble much off the ends because they were so full of food already. This time Majel told them about a place where she used to play with other children when she was a little girl in the Middle West. It was a junk pile in a gravel pit, with a lot of old stoves and stovepipes that the children put together in all sorts of funny ways, to make rooms and twisty tunnels up and down.

Then one day the children brought all the cats they

could find and coaxed and pushed them into the stove-pipes. All the cats, tiger-striped and marmalade, calico and gray, came out at the other end very black cats indeed. The funniest had been a spoiled and haughty white angora who belonged to a Mrs. Perkins who lived across the road. The angora always wore a pale blue silk bow round her neck, but when she got out of the stovepipe she was dressed up in a black bow and black fur coat. When Mrs. Perkins opened her front door and called, "Annabelle—here, Annabelle!" a black cat answered her. Mrs. Perkins slammed her door shut in a hurry, but Annabelle got in through the window.

"I can't tell you how Mrs. Perkins screamed with fear," Majel said, "and we screamed with joy! Annabelle changed colors for days after that—from black to dark gray to light gray to plain dirty. It was a long time before she was white again."

How the three boys laughed! They thought Majel was wonderful. "Majel's day" was a big event in Em's and Dwi's lives every year. But now they had to go to bed.

When Majel left that night, there hung on the wall, next to the blue window, a beautiful stained-glass cross with a tin frame. It was Majel's second Christmas present to Bea.

The next day the whole family was cutting and hammering tin stars, fish, hearts and crosses. It was surely going to be a fine, fantastic Christmas tree this year.

5. Christmas Eve

More people came to the Rancho Arroyo to help with the Christmas preparations. Some of them Nils did not know, but he liked them all, and it was lots of fun.

Already the boys had half filled thirty paper sacks with sand, and their grown-up friends Dick and Ruby had been up on the roof making the Christmas illuminations called *luminarios*. It seemed strange to Nils that the roofs

53

here in New Mexico were flat. Dick and Ruby fixed a candle into the sand in each paper bag and spaced the bags round the edges of the roofs. The candles would be lit tomorrow for Christmas Eve, so the Christ Child could see where the boys' home was and find His way to their hearts.

Hilario had to stack a big pile of wood for a bonfire outside the house. All the farmers nearby did the same thing. "They do it in town, in Santa Fe, too," he told Nils.

Now they were indoors. The fire crackled on the hearth, filling the room with a lovely smell of pine. In the corner between the blue window and the chimney stood the Christmas tree, waiting to be dressed with the shining ornaments they were making for it.

The red table was covered with all sorts of paper— gold and silver and every possible color. Round the table sat Lena and the boys, Margaret, Dick, Ruby, Bea, and Graeme, another of her old friends. Dwi was very busy stringing popcorn and raisins into long garlands. Ruby and Graeme were making silver-paper angels, and Bea made a gorgeous big gold one for the top of the tree. Nils showed them how to make heart baskets in two colors, and these were filled with candy.

Before the guests drove off to Santa Fe, the boys had a very busy time for a while. Em had forgotten to shut the little gate beside the cattle-guard, and suddenly the alfalfa field was full of horses and cows. The three boys chased them round the whole rancho, with Silver running alongside, barking. Up hill and down the horses went, and at last they jumped over the fence like deer. Nils thought that Em was just like those horses, small and thin, but very fast and full of pep. The cows were a funny breed, all with white faces. Bea said they always just stood and slept on the roads at night, so Nils thought maybe they had those white faces so that they could better be seen.

After all the excitement and all that exercise, the boys were very tired when they went to bed. Nils turned his little pocket flashlight on the angel over Em's bed; it was a nice way to use a flashlight.

"Shall we say our evening prayer, all three of us together, while I keep the light shining on the angel?" he asked. So the three boys said their prayers. Em and Dwi said:

> *Now I lay me down to sleep,*
> *I pray the Lord my soul to keep.*

If I should die before I wake,
I pray the Lord my soul to take.

Nils said his prayer in Danish:

> Jeg er traet jeg gaar til Ro
> lukker mine Ojne to
> se O Herre venlig ned
> til mit lille Lejested.

In English that means:

> *I am tired and go to rest,*
> *Closing my two eyes.*
> *Thou, O Lord, look kindly down*
> *On my little nest.*

And quickly Nils put in a little private prayer: "Mother, come soon, please!"

Then Nils turned off his light, but the boys talked until Lena came and said, "You have to go to sleep now —no more talking. Tomorrow night you will be up very late. The Christ Child is coming tomorrow." She had brought a little golden angel with blue wings that she put on a shelf, and she lighted a vigil light inside it. "Good night, boys," she said.

It was Christmas Eve. Dick and the boys were up on the roof, lighting the luminarios. It was snowing a little, but the candles were burning beautifully. Hilario lit the big pitchwood bonfire outside the door to help the Christ child find His way. One by one, all the other farms were illuminated, and everywhere on the hills they could see the lights on roofs and fires outside the doors.

The Christmas tree was dressed with all the gold and silver birds and fish. All of Nils' hearts were filled with chocolate, tiny toys, or nuts. Popcorn garlands swung from branch to branch, and little surprises were tucked in everywhere. There were a Santa Claus, an Indian drum, a little auto, all the tin stars and crosses and fishes they had made with Majel—everywhere there was something new!

Under the tree were the gifts, a big, big pile of packages. And in front of the fireplace hung a row of stockings.

"What's that for?" Nils asked. "What do you use stockings for?"

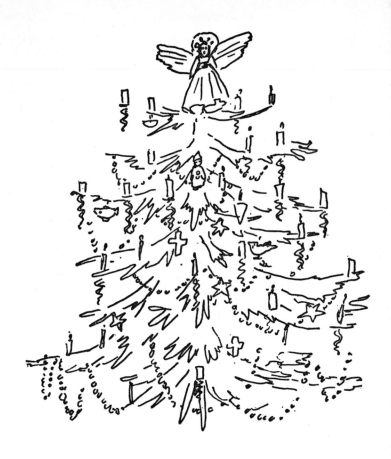

"Don't you know?" said Dwi. "They are for Santa Claus to fill. He is coming tonight in his sleigh with reindeer. He comes down the chimney and fills our stockings with presents." He felt very big to be able to teach big Nils something.

Singing began outside the house. The boys peeped out of the window to see children and grownups out there singing carols. The bonfire lighted up their faces, and big flakes of snow were falling down on them.

Nils was allowed to light the Christmas tree. It was covered all over with tiny electric blubs—red, blue, green, and yellow. Nils had never seen anything like it before. Bing! You plugged in one wire and the whole tree blazed. He thought that was very smart.

Nils remembered his last Christmas Eve in Denmark. Mother and Father always dressed the tree secretly, and Nils and Baby Bix had to wait on the other side of the door with their very best clothes on. Then, suddenly— the door was opened, and they looked at a beautiful sight. Mother Ida had a different kind of tree every year for them. That last one had been a silver spruce. Mother had put lots of heavy cotton on the branches, and over it a lot of salt with diamond dust in it. Long icicles hung from every branch, and the cones were all of silver. Baskets and cornucopias held nuts and fruit and marzipan. All over the tree real little white candles flickered. How Nils loved those flames! Then Santa Claus came in, in a red coat and red cap and big boots. He came with a sled filled with Christmas gifts. Nils and Bix called him

Julemanden. Nils knew very well it was his father, but it was very exciting just the same.

Nils sighed now, remembering. Looking at the beautiful New Mexican Christmas tree, he thought about his long voyage. Everything was lovely here in the adobe house, with the fireplace and the black cross on the wall, and the long red table with all the Christmas fruit. If Mother were only here, or Father!

More cars came, and more people gathered outside. The boys went out to sing carols with them, all their faces wet and shining with melting snow. They sang:

Silent night, holy night,
All is calm, all is bright
Round yon Virgin Mother and Child;
Holy Infant, so tender and mild,
Sleep in heavenly peace.

After the carol, Bea invited everyone in to see the Christmas tree and have hot tea and all sorts of cookies. Graeme arrived, and Margaret, and Dick and Ruby, and the pile of gifts grew into a regular mountain.

Most of the guests went off to sing carols at other ranchos, and then Graeme and Margaret played carols on the violin and flute. They all ate chicken salad and sandwiches. But the presents were still under the Christmas tree.

"Tomorrow," said Bea.

"Oh—tomorrow," Nils thought. Different places, different ways.

At last all the guests had gone except Margaret, and the boys really should have been in bed. But this evening they could stay up a little later. The fire threw long, mysterious red lights across the room, gleaming on the long table with its candlesticks and the basket of fruit between them that held pears and apples, grapes and oranges and nuts. Em and Dwi sat on the hearth on one side of the fire, and Nils on the other. Bea was sharing Trusty's blue Mexican chair. Margaret perched on a little red stool, and Lena sat in the wooden chair. They all felt that it was lovely just to sit there, quietly looking at the Christmas tree and the fire.

Bea suggested, "Let's each of us tell a Christmas story."

The boys moved together, so that the three of them were like a clover leaf. The snow pattered softly against the windows. The pitchwood bonfire was still burning outside, and the candles fought hard to keep alight against the wind so the Christ Child could see that it was His birthday at the Rancho Arroyo.

It was really a holy night! Everybody felt it. And now to tell Christmas stories! Stories were some of the best things in the little ranch boys' lives.

Bea began with the story about the Christ Child.

"It is a very old story, nearly two thousand years old. It happened in Palestine, where there are no Christmas trees, no firs or pines, only palm trees. There was born a little Child in the town of Bethlehem, and at that moment a big, beautiful star shone in the sky. All the people saw it. The shepherds saw it, and kings saw it. It was a sign.

"Three holy kings came with gifts and incense to worship the Child they said was the King of the World. Herod, the evil king in Jerusalem heard about it, and he wanted no other king to be his rival. He ordered his soldiers to kill all the boy babies under two years old—"

"I am nearly five years old," Dwi said quickly.

"And I am seven," said Em.

"Good for you!" said Bea. "But Joseph, the little Child's father, dreamed that he should take his wife and baby and go out of the country. So he did. The Christ Child rode in His mother's arms on a burro, and Joseph walked alongside, and they reached Egypt safely. So the Christ Child was saved from the wicked king, and since that time everybody has a fire outside his house so the Child can find His way."

After the story the big basket of fruit had to be passed round, and Lena had a pitcher of lemonade to fill the glasses.

"Now, how about Nils?" Bea asked. "Can you tell us a story?"

"Yes," said Nils. "I was as big as Dwi— No, I was

still smaller, only four years old. I remembered just a little about how a Christmas tree had to look, and for a whole month before Christmas I worked on one of my own. I collected all the tinfoil I could find, little pieces along the road and even in the ditch. I collected stubs of candles, too. I had seen how my mother made candles. She melted all the little bits together, and dipped cotton strings up and down, up and down in the wax.

"So when Christmas Eve came I had seven candles. I made little baskets and cornucopias out of colored paper from a scrapbook, and covered little potatoes with tinfoil, and fir cones too. I made flowers out of colored paper, and some chains like the ones Dwi made. I made a big star out of pieces of tin boxes cut in long points.

"On Christmas Eve we were invited to a village for the tree there. But I hurried away from our house to have my own tree first. I went out into the forest and found a most beautiful little spruce, exactly right, with stiff, flat blue branches. It was three o'clock and already getting to be twilight. I dressed up my little tree with the big star at the top, and all the baskets filled with little bits of potatoes and grain and seeds scattered on the branches. I fastened my seven little candles on with wire.

"To make it still more beautiful, the snow began to

fall, little flakes at first, then larger and larger. I lighted the candles, and the little tree looked like a dream. It was so still there in the wood I could hear the snow falling on the branches—*puff, puff, puff*. I must have looked like a snowman myself when I sang the carol I had known since I was two years old. It was "Silent Night," the same one we sang here tonight, but I sang it in Danish. I sang it all alone for my little tree that was now pure white, with shining stars and lights like diamonds.

"I blew out the candles and ran home just in time to have my hot Christmas bath, which was something special. Then I put my Sunday clothes on and my big boots, and off we went. It was snowy and windy, and we had to walk two miles to the village.

"At the town hall I was given warm milk and Christmas muffins. But I was so tired from the wind and snow that the warm room made me very sleepy. The next morning I couldn't remember one single thing about the big tree there. But I still had my own little tree in the forest that nobody else knew anything about.

"When I went out to see it again, I heard a lot of peeping and cheeping from quite far away. Imagine! I found that tree full of birds—tomtits and titmice and sparrows, all eating the seeds in the baskets and pecking

at the candles. Two rabbits were sitting up, nibbling at the silvered potatoes. Oh, it was a real festival!

"The snow was full of footprints of birds and animals that had already been there to the Christmas party. I was amazed. Can you imagine, I hadn't known I had made a Christmas Eve for the animals! When I came closer, the birds flew up into big trees nearby and made a great concert. My, how they chirped and cheeped. I was sure they were saying, '*Tak for Mal.*' That means, 'Thanks for the meal.'

"I lighted what was left of the candles, and my Christmas tree looked to me as if it were smiling. I smiled too, and decided that I would do that every year. Every year I would make the birds a Christmas tree, and the rabbits could eat the candles if some were left. And I always do it."

"A birds' Christmas tree!" exclaimed Em. "We'll do that first thing tomorrow morning. We can easily find a tree out here."

Bea said it was bedtime for the boys, but Dwi put his arms round Lena's neck. "Lena, *you* tell us a story before we go to bed." His velvet-brown eyes were big and round, and Lena, for all her common sense, could never hold out long against Dwi.

"All right, Bea, let me tell the boys just one more little story, and Christmas Eve will be over.

"Last Christmas Eve I thought I would like to go to midnight Mass at the San Ildefonso church. I thought that afterward the Indians would dance in the church.

"It was snowing, just as it is tonight, but Grace came over from the dude ranch to go with me. It was all right until we came to the Nambe river bed, and then Pegasus began to dance like an Indian war dancer, from one side of the road to the other. I was scared because of course I didn't want to smash Bea's car.

"It was dark and stormy, and we hopped like that all the way to San Ildefonso. I drove through a lot of mud, but as we got near the church something went wrong inside the car, and the motor stopped. We saw a big fire outside the church, with a lot of Indians warming their backs at it. We went across the plaza to it; the night was dark, and it was so muddy that Grace lost her rubber.

"When we got to the church we were pretty dirty; there was hardly anybody there—only two Indian women in blankets. We were glad, though, that fires were roaring in the two big stoves. Time went on and on—one o'clock, two o'clock, three, then four. Finally some more Indians and some Spanish Americans came in. Then Lucia and her sister and two friends came, and we sat with them in their pew.

"It was half past four when the priest came. The Mass was beautiful, and all the people went to the altar rail to receive Communion. Then the priest lifted up a Christ

Child of painted wood, as big as a real baby, and the people at the rail all kissed the Child—and the service was over.

"It was after five o'clock, and everybody went home. We started to wait for the Indian dance, but somebody told us the Indians weren't going to dance that year. I thought of Pegasus waiting out in the mud. A little disappointed at our lost Christmas Eve, we went out to find the car. But the fire outdoors had gone out, and we couldn't see anything at all. Grace slipped in the mud because she couldn't see. Lucia lost one shoe. It was as dark as the inside of an ink bottle, and we kept calling and shouting to one another.

"We couldn't even find the car. Lucia called, 'Juanito, help! Lena can't find her car.' Then a flashlight flicked round, and there stood Pegasus, sleeping, with his eyes shut."

Dwi giggled. "What happened then?" Em asked.

"We got in, but Pegasus wouldn't go. I asked Lucia's friend Juanito to give us a push. He did, and Pegasus ran as quick as he could, right down into a mud hole! Juanito pushed and pushed; then he got stuck in the mud. 'Lucia, come!' he called. 'You are freezing with only one shoe on.' He told us he would take Lucia home first.

"With a big noise he finally got out of the mud and disappeared. We were alone, left in the mud in the dark. It stormed and blew, and there was nobody to be seen in all that dark. When I saw a flashlight far away across the plaza, I yelled like an Indian. 'Hi-i-i-i! I am stuck in the mud.' A few doors opened; then they shut again.

"So then I gave another Indian whoop—a big one, I can tell you! 'Hi-i-i-i! Hi-i-i-i!' It echoed through the whole pueblo. A lot of flashlights appeared from adobe houses near and far away. It snowed and blew, and I kept on calling in the dark.

"We heard people coming, and now and then they flashed their lights to see where the calls were coming from. We could not see who they were, but they were speaking the Indian language. I kept calling to them, 'I can't leave this car—it's not mine and I have to get it home!'

"When they reached the car and took hold of it, they were on the warpath. 'Hi, yi, yi!' they yelled. You can talk as much as you like about Indians being serious in the daytime, but that Christmas Eve they were certainly full of fun. 'Hi-yi-yi!' they yelled and fell in the mud. 'Hi-yi-yi!'—and they were up again, pushing and pulling. 'Hi-yi-yi!' Those Indians lifted the car right up out of the mud and ran, pushing it. We could hear them as they disappeared uphill with poor Pegasus. Then one Indian must have got in, because we heard *put-put-put-putput!* Up onto the dry road it ran, and we cheered and scurried to catch up. We were afraid the engine would die again when we got in, so we couldn't take time over our thankyous. The Indians called, 'Merry Christmas!' after us, and we called back, 'Merry Christmas!' So we left them and they must have been muddied right up to the necks of their Christmas clothes. The sun was rising over the Sangre de Cristo mountains when we got back here to the rancho."

"So you were out the whole night, Lena?" Em and Dwi laughed. "That was a funny story."

Then the three boys said good night and Merry Christmas, and off they went to their own house to bed. It had been a lovely Christmas Eve.

6. Christmas Day

Ding dong! Ding dong! It was six o'clock in the morning when Lena wakened the boys with her big bell. "Hey, boys, Santa Claus has been here. The Festival is beginning at seven. All men on deck!"

The boys scurried up to the bathroom with their clothes under their arms. They had to be nice and clean for Christmas morning.

The red table was set with candles and fruit and flowers, and rows of the beautiful Mexican cups and plates. Lena brought steaming hot muffins, and Ruby came in with a huge platter of bacon and eggs. There was oatmeal cake, which Nils called "sister cake." The fire roared in the chimney and smelled of pitch, and the tree was lighted.

After breakfast Uncle Dick was the master of ceremonies and gave out presents. He read the little verses on all the packages, and each person had to thank him with a two-line verse. There were heaps of gifts, trains and footballs and baseballs and baseball gloves—too many things to count. Nils thought there was enough for a whole country.

Nils gave Em a little pocket flashlight like his own. Bea got a Danish royal porcelain girl with a red skirt that Nils' father had bought in Copenhagen. And Nils gave Dwi a box with hammer and saw and screwdriver and nails.

"Goodness," said Bea, "don't you use that in the house, Dwight."

"No, Bea," Dwi promised, "only out in the piano box."

They had more coffee, more muffins, more ham and

eggs, more toast and marmalade. The Festival went on and on, because all yesterday's guests had left armfuls of gifts under the tree. As soon as the boys passed the rhyme test, it all went quickly. Cups and dishes, cakes and muffins, the coffee pot and spoons all disappeared in a deluge of colored papers, ribbons, and boxes.

When Nils was handed the Christmas picture-letter from Mother that he was waiting for, he didn't hear any of the laughter round him for a while. Mother had painted it just for Father and him; looking at it, Nils dreamed himself back to see Mother sitting at her work table, making all those little drawings and thinking about him. He could feel her love streaming out from the paper. There was Father as Santa Claus; and Bix, looking a little bigger than he remembered, and with longer hair, was looking at the tree. "Forget me not," it said underneath that picture. As if Nils or Father ever could forget!

Then there was Mother with the candles for the dinner table. She was wearing the Swedish costume she brought with her from Grandy's house after she got married and came to live in Denmark. How well Nils remembered how *that* table looked on Christmas! Flags trimmed it—and tiny Swedish wooden dolls, straw goats, and straw angels set out on a long runner with green reeds

and hearts. There were snowmen and red Swedish horses
with candles in their saddles; bottles with hearts and
flourishes and small dancers on them. The napkins had
dancers on them, and the jugs for the Christmas beer and
the plates had a queen in the middle and ornaments
round the borders. Such a painter Mother was—she had
put it all into her picture! There she was in the corner
herself. Nils kissed her—then quickly he jumped down
from his pink cloud. Had anyone seen him be so silly?
No, no one had; they were still all unwrapping more gifts
and laughing.

Nils put the painted Christmas letter carefully back
into its envelope and joined the others. This was a different kind of Christmas, but it was fun too. The Christmas
tree was really different, but it was nice that they had
made everything for it with their own hands. If only
Mother and Father could be here to see it!

Nils' sigh was lost in the noise of a new game the boys
were playing with a huge sack they called the Wishing
Well. They put in their hands and grabbed a package.
Sometimes they got a potato or a piece of soap, sometimes a box of chocolate or a toy.

When Nils grabbed he got a bottle of perfume, and he
laughed so hard he nearly fell off his red stool. It was

good to laugh like that. Uncle Dick picked out a red rose, and the house nearly rocked off the hill when he put it behind his ear. Ruby told funny stories in between grabs. They had a Tee-hee's egg in a Ha-ha's nest and were all going up Fool's Hill.

Then Lena called, "It's still snowing, boys! But you'd better get the good of it before it melts away. It may only be here for another hour or two."

The boys put on their sweaters and rubber boots, and Dwi wore his new red gloves. Down they flew to the storeroom to drag the sled out from behind the coal sacks. Lots of boxes had to be moved and turned over—but never mind that today. They did not want to waste another minute of the snow. They left the door open behind them because it was blocked with boxes, and the snow blew in over the coal and wood.

What a jolly time they had rushing up and down old Pegasus's hill, with Pegasus himself watching them from under his nightcap of snow! Lena came out, dressed in the ski suit she used to wear at home in Vermont. She knew all about snow and sleds. She and the boys lay on their stomachs on the sled and rushed like a blizzard the whole way down to the cattle-guard. It was a wonderful snowy Christmas day for those little desert boys!

When it was Nils' turn, he took the sled in his arms and ran up the hill to the cottonwood, nearly up to the Indian land. He threw himself onto the sled as he put it down, and off he went, full speed like an arrow, down Pegasus's hill, over the cattle-guard, and all the way to Señor Pedro's place at the bend in the arroyo. Señor Pedro's wife, who could speak only Spanish, saw Nils' grand finish. So did little Carolina, the sweetest little Spanish girl in the whole Pojoaque Valley. She had two big black braids and big brown eyes and a red dress, and she was always smiling. Nils was glad she had seen how fine he was on the sled.

When he got back up the hill, Lena told him that not even a Vermonter could have done better. The Garcia boys wanted to try it alone, but now the sun had come out and the snow was melting, leaving bare patches. It was one o'clock, and Bea was calling them in to dinner.

"Now we shall all take a nap," said Bea, after they were all so full that they could not eat a single bite more. "Something is going to happen tonight!"

Em squirmed in his seat. "What is it, Bea? I am not sleepy."

But Bea wouldn't tell them what it was and said that even if they weren't sleepy they were to go to bed now. She finally got the boys off to their beds, though they were still guessing at what the surprise was going to be. And they were sleeping like stones when Lena came down the hill after helping Bea clear away the dinner. The whole rancho slept. Even Bea got a nap.

It was ten o'clock at night when Bea woke them with the bell. *Bing-bang! Bing-bang!* They felt that they could sleep for seventeen more hours, but Bea wouldn't hear of anything like that. "Lena has hot coffee for all of us, and sister cake." Bea had started now to call the Christmas cake by its Danish name.

Coffee! That was different. They only got coffee on birthday mornings. They were out of bed in a jiffy.

"No bath," Bea told them.

That made it even more special. No bath, and coffee—

Em couldn't figure out the reason for all this strangeness. He was out of the door and up the wet earth staircase and in the kitchen before Nils or Dwi was half dressed.

He saw Dick's car. "What's up, Dick?" he asked.

But before Dick could answer, Bea had something to say. She saw that Em wasn't wearing stockings. He was to go back down immediately and put on long woolen stockings and his long plaid trousers and coveralls. He was to bring his heavy coat and warm cap, his red neckerchief and mittens, and tell the other boys to do the same. It was no use complaining when Bea had that face on, so off went Em with the new orders.

Ten minutes later they were all sitting round the long table with very red cheeks, eating their oatmeal sister cake and drinking steaming hot coffee from mugs. Then came the news!

"We are going to the Christmas Festival at San Ildefonso. The Indians are going to dance in the church tonight!"

Two cars set off in the dark cold night. On their way out of the arroyo they saw a thin animal in the glare of the headlights.

"Is it Silver?" Nils asked. Then he saw another gray

shape, and another. Up on the Reservation there was a sharp bark, then an answering howl. It made Nils' skin prickle with fear. "Is it—is it wolves?" he wanted to know.

"Not wolves—coyotes," Bea said.

Em and Dwi told Nils about coyotes, how they were not at all as terrible as wolves and really were a help to the farmers, keeping down the rodents that did damage on the ranchos. They might look frightening and sound frightening, but really they were useful creatures in their way. Nils did not say so, but he still did not want to meet any coyotes when he was not in a car with other people.

When they came to San Ildefonso they could see the Festival from far away. Hundreds of big and small fires were burning all round, just as they had last night, and on the plaza was a special big fire so that the whole tall cottonwood tree that stood there glowed red. Outside the church two Indians were on guard with guns. They kept shooting up into the air to keep the evil spirits away from the church.

At midnight the church bell rang and Indians came out of their houses, wrapped in colorful blankets. Their black hair shone in the light, but they did not say a word and only the crackling of the pitchwood could be heard

and the shots when the two guards fired again. Then the
church doors were shut behind them.

After the bell called again and the watchmen shot
into the air, the doors opened again.

Father Antonio came out, dressed in his vestments,
followed by six altar boys carry censers and candles. Then
came six Indians, carrying the holy San Francisco and
San Ildefonso under a canopy. The priest prayed and was
answered by all the Indians, and they followed him and

the Saints all round the big plaza and then round the second plaza. At last everyone went into the church, which was warmed by two stoves with pipes as long as an evil day. All the Indians knelt down. The two watching Indians shot into the air once more, and the church was closed.

Father Antonio went up to the altar and knelt there. Then he lifted the wooden Christ Child from His cradle and held Him in his arms like a real baby. Every Indian went up to the altar rail and kissed the Child, happy and silent. Not a sound could be heard except the priest's voice giving the blessing.

At one o'clock the Indians danced the Eagle Dance in the church. Four dancers with big eagle wings made the movements of a bird in flight, in camp, in victory, and in joy. The dance was beautiful, and the church was exactly the right background for it.

7. "I Can Hear the Drums
over the Mountains"

The days went on, and snow fell on the mountaintops.
Some of Bea's artist friends went to California. It was
too cold for them in Pojoaque. When Em and little Dwi
went back to their school after the Christmas holidays,
Nils went with them.

This school seemed a peculiar one to the Danish boy.

There were forty pupils and four classes all in one room. At the same time one class had writing, another algebra, a third drawing, and a fourth history—and there was only one teacher for all.

Nils was told that it was a "progressive school," but he was surprised to find that what the children did mostly was just play. Nils made himself useful helping the teacher, showing pupils how to mold clay into animal shapes, how to draw a cat or a bird, just as his mother had taught him. It was all fun, but he longed for a real school where he would have to work hard.

Every day the hours seemed longer. Then one afternoon Bea gave him a letter that Mother had written on Christmas Eve, and time did not exist any more for a while.

Holte, Christmas Eve

My dear big son,

I got your letter from the train and also the one from the boat. I am so glad you sent them Air Mail so that they reached me for Christmas.

You really are getting grown up and I can see you are making many friends. I am glad that you found both Rannveig and Margaret. The world is not such a big place after all.

It is Christmas Eve. Bix is in bed now, and I would like to have a little talk with you. We had a *little* Christmas tree this year, with all the things from last year's tree, so you know just how it looked. This is not the time to spend money if it isn't necessary. Bix was happy, but she is always asking for Father and Nils. I tell her as much as I can, because I do not want her to forget you.

Bix got a nice warm dress that I knitted myself. It will be good to have if we suddenly have to leave for America. She got a cape, too, and a pair of mittens. Edna gave her a toy dog and Peder brought her fur gloves.

I got a book—*The Yearling*. I have read a little of it already, and I can imagine my Nils having a deer just like the one in the book. We sang "Happy Christmas" and had our Christmas meal at six o'clock. It was a little lonesome, but beautiful. There were candles and flowers, and duck with apples and prunes inside, nuts and dates, and even an orange, Nils.

You tell me to come over to America with Baby right away, but I still do not have all the papers, and I haven't sold the house yet. I will try to get over to Grandy's in Sweden to talk things over with him. But in the meantime we are packing. Bix is always coming with something I must put in for her. If I say there is no room she just asks, "Don't you want to *rescue* that doll? And that dog?" As if they had to be saved from a deluge. I am going to put her in kindergarten until we are ready to leave. That way I can get more done and she will have other children to play with. I will bring her home every evening at five.

I am doing my best to get over to you. You know that, Nils. Good night, and love and Christmas kisses to my big son.

Mother Ida

There was nothing Nils wanted so much as to have his mother and Bix here right away. But he knew he had to wait—and wait.

"Hush!" said Bea one evening. "Listen!" She whispered, "I can hear the drums over the mountains."

The boys all listened: *Drum*—drumdrum—*drum*—drumdrum . . .

"What, is it the twenty-second of January already? Then it is San Geronimo Day tomorrow—the big buffalo dance! They have already started. Now, boys, what about it? Do you want to go? If you do, nobody goes to school tomorrow, you know."

Nils was all afire to go to find the drummers, but Em loved his school, so he said, "We can go to school in the afternoon, can't we, Bea?"

"You, Emerson, you can go to school. We'll go after the drums," said Bea.

"I guess I'd rather go with you, Bea." Em laughed.

"Then early to bed with you," said Bea. "We start from here at five o'clock."

At seven that evening all three boys were asleep down in their caboose.

Snow fell during the night. It was dark and cold at five in the morning, but the boys were lively and eating a good hot breakfast. At a quarter past five they bumped off down the arroyo in Pegasus.

When they came out on the road to Ildefonso they could no longer hear the drums. They could not hear the drums even when they drove up to the plaza.

"You know, boys, this is the Indians' most holy dance, so don't make a sound, please!"

"Where are they?" whispered Em.

They listened. There was not a sound, not even a whisper of wind in the cottonwood tree. Everything was pitch dark—not a light in a single window. It was a sleeping town.

Bea set out to investigate, and the three boys followed her like beads on a string.

"Can it be that it was yesterday, not today?" Nils whispered.

"No, it's today, as soon as the sky gets red, but we have to find them in the dark. Now, quiet, boys!" Bea's voice was as low as Nils'.

Very silently they went down the road to the second plaza, along a row of poplars. Nils couldn't help feeling nervous—the Indians might be behind the trees. They could be in any of the little alleyways. Bea waited and listened. Even Dwi was as mute as a fish. Then a dog barked in a house.

A little smoke rose from a chimney, curling into air that was paling to gray. Snow covered everything, and it was very cold. A woman slipped out to a well and got a pail of water. She disappeared again without a sound.

"Where are they?"

They listened again. Nothing. Yes: *hum*—humhum
—very, very softly. Where did it come from? *Hum*—
humhum . . .

Suddenly there they stood—eight Indians in a row, as
if they had grown in a moment out of the earth. Nils'
hair rose on his head. It was magic—sorcery. Nobody
made a sound. The boys didn't even move.

The Indians were very, very ancient men, their faces
like maps with thousands of wrinkles. They had long hair
with ribbons braided in, white skin trousers, and big
bright-colored blankets over their shoulders. Each had a
big drum—except for one, who looked like a chieftain
and stood with his arms folded against his chest. The
others seemed barely to touch their drums, and the sound
came as if from far away: *thum*—thumthum—*thum*—
thumthum. They looked as if they were carved out of
stone.

Suddenly, on top of the closest foothill of the Jemez
Mountains, a little fire appeared. Against the small red
spot something was moving—was it coyotes? Nils wondered; but no, it was creatures with horns, moving slowly
downward.

The sky was showing a little color, but the air seemed

colder and colder. Horns showed against the sky now. They came closer and closer—not silent now, but with the *ding-ding-ding* of silver bells. The drums grew louder: *Drum*—drumdrum—*Drum*—drumdrum. Then they came, Indians dressed up as deer, with big horns and two sticks for forelegs. Behind them were hunters in red and blue velvet blouses.

The sky reddened as the drivers passed the drummers, driving the herd of deer down to the big Indian kiva that had no windows at all, and no door except in the roof. Every man, woman, and child in the pueblo had come out in colorful ceremonial costume and followed the drummers and the chief.

Then the dance started. It was the deer dance. They danced the hunting dance—hunters, drivers, and deer together. The sky was redder, and the snow looked blue. Then the dance ended. The sky glowed with red, purple, and yellow, and the deer disappeared into the kiva.

Nils looked at the sun coming up with a great splash of light over the mountain range. It was wonderful. He turned to see the Indians who had been spectators. Where were they? They had disappeared as if by magic again—not a single one to be seen. It might be sorcery, Nils thought.

There was not a sound now. Bea and the three boys stood alone on the dead, silent plaza. It had been wonderful. They tiptoed over to Pegasus.

When they got home to the Rancho Arroyo, they heard again the drums over the mountains—silver bells and drums. The Indians danced for three days.

8. Bea's Birthday

It was Bea's birthday, and she and Lena had gone to Ruby's house in Santa Fe. It was a luncheon party just for grownups, so the boys had to stay home. Em and Dwi were not happy about that, and they were not much interested in the landscapes they were painting at the red table.

Nils sat down at the other end, writing a letter to his mother. He was not happy either, but it was not because

Bea and Lena weren't there to cheer them up. He was lonely for his mother. He felt badly, too, because he had not written to her as often as he ought. Sometimes it seemed as if the more homesick and lonely he was inside, the harder it was to get out pen and paper and talk to her in a letter.

Dear Mother Ida and Bix,

I miss you so awfully much that it hurts down in my fingers and even out in my toes. Can't you come right away? I have not seen Father since I left the station in Chicago, but I get letters from him sometimes. He tells me he is still working on some flood gates up in Colorado. But maybe he will be going to study something in the Bear Mountain in California, where Uncle Stürstrom is. Do you remember I met Uncle Stürstrom on the *Gripsholm* coming to America? He is a naturalist and goes all over the world collecting plants.

Father writes that if he does go to California I am to move to San Bernardino, where he can see me more often. Maybe I am to stay with Uncle Piper, who is living in some mountains near there. He is Swedish, and we saw him one summer at Leksand, do you remember? I always thought he was a strange fellow because he lived in the hills in a cabin all alone, but he taught me how to use a knife to carve animals in wood. Father says he lives most of the day in a tower in California, but he still makes figures out of wood. I want to be closer to Father so we can see each other, but I shall miss Em and Dwi. Most of the time they are funny and make me laugh a lot.

You should see how I am growing. I think the food must be doing it because Bea is always talking about calories and vitamins. We get orange juice every day and often grapefruit—can you imagine? Bea cuts the grapefruit in the evening and fills a hole in the middle with honey. By morning they have soaked up the honey and taste wonderful. We drink goat's milk that Patches gives us. I didn't like it at first, but now I like the taste better than real cow's milk.

But at night when I am in bed I always think about you. I got so homesick one time I didn't sleep the whole night. Come soon, or I will be so big you won't know me. My clothes are already tight for me.

I am so unhappy today. There is a snowstorm, and all the little horses out on the Indian land stand with their backs to the wind, so all their hair blows in front of them. They look very miserable, and lonesome for a warm stable too. Even Em and Dwi aren't funny today, because it is Bea's birthday and she is away.

Em and Dwi quarreled about the blue paint. Then they went to the icebox to see if there was anything to eat in it. They ate the lunch Bea left too early, so they can't wait for supper. Bea does not like them to go to the icebox, but Em doesn't care, if he's hungry. Now they have come back. They found some chicken legs and some hard-boiled eggs. They ate them and gave me one egg and went back to the kitchen house again. I can hear them talking about me. "You didn't give Nils any chicken," Dwi said. "He is not as hungry as I am," Em said. "Here's something in this jar—oh, pears!" "Don't," Dwi said, but Em said they were good.

They haven't said anything more out there for quite a while. I am sure all that food was for our supper tonight, and what will Bea and Lena say when they come back? Em called to me to come out if I was hungry. I said I wasn't, but I *am*. There is something going on outdoors—it is Pegasus chugging up the hill. So I will close now with kisses for you and Bix.

Your big son, Nils

Bea came in and found the icebox open. Poor Bea; it was still her birthday, and she had had a bad time getting back. With all the snow, Pegasus had barely made it. Now there was the icebox open, and the milk would

probably be sour. "Did you forget to close it?" she asked
Lena.

Lena rushed to the icebox. "Bea, those boys have eaten
the eggs—and the chicken—and the dessert."

Bea and Lena could see that the icebox was practically
empty. The boys stood and looked at her, their eyes big
with guilt.

Dwi said, "I—I only ate *one* egg—and o-one l-l-leg."

Bea looked in the icebox again. "And the pears?" she
asked.

"Yes, the pears," whispered Dwi.

Bea went over to the sink corner, and Em began to
yell. He knew she was getting the stick.

Dwi's dark brown eyes got bigger and bigger, and his
cheeks got redder and redder. He knew that Em would
scream his head off, and he couldn't stand hearing Em
scream. "I ate everything, Bea!" he cried. "I took it all,
Bea!" He ran across to stand between Bea and Em and
get the spanking for both of them.

"Em, stop that screaming!" Bea shouted. "I haven't
spanked you yet."

"But you want to!" Em really looked very pitiful—and
he knew it, the imp.

Bea looked at both of them. "Go to bed," she said. "There is nothing to eat. You have had all our supper."

The boys knew that Bea meant it. But they were sure that there was something good in Pegasus's rumble seat, because Bea never came back from Santa Fe without food. They put on their coats and went out in the snowy dark, down the hill to their little house. Lena let them take the flashlight, but she did not follow them as she usually did when they went to bed in the dark.

Nils picked up his coat too. But Bea said, "Stay here, Nils, you haven't done anything wrong."

"Yes, I did," Nils said. "I ate an egg."

"Never mind," said Bea. "You wait. Let them go alone. I know Emerson."

Nils sat down. He felt very ashamed and would rather have gone with the boys. After all, he was nearly ten years old—a big boy—and Em was only seven and Dwi still littler. He could have stopped them from being bad, but he had been thinking only of his letter to Mother Ida. And what would Mother think about him if she knew?

Bea put on her raincoat and covered her hair with a bathing cap. Lena just wore a coat. Her hair always curled in rain or snow, so she never minded getting it wet.

Pegasus was still standing steaming outside, and they brought in piles of parcels. All sorts of good things sprouted out of big bags and brown boxes—*everything*, even packages with ribbons, even a birthday cake with nine candles left—three for each boy. Nils thought it was terrible that Bea's pleasure was all spoiled when she had brought all that for the boys.

Nils went into the sitting room and folded the pages of his letter. He cleared the table and put the cap on the ink bottle. He took as much time as he could about it, with his back to the kitchen, so Bea would not see he was having to swallow a big lump in his throat.

"Come, Nils," Bea called. "Take this." She had fixed a tray for him. It had a plate of sandwiches and salad, and a glass of goat's milk and some candy on it. There was a piece of birthday cake with three candles.

And Lena said, "Sit down in the sitting room. Eat it slowly. It isn't good for you to hurry. Let's give him an apple, Bea."

"May I eat it down in the boys' house?" Nils asked in a small voice. He thought there would be something for all three of them that way.

Bea came in and sat down in Trusty's chair and said,

"You know, Lena, I think they have had punishment enough. I really had looked forward to ending my birthday with a party for the boys. Shall we let them come up when we have the table ready?"

Lena looked surprised. She thought it was a dangerous thing to do. Em was such a clever boy, he would be sure to understand Bea's weakness. Then she relented too. After all, it *was* Bea's birthday, and maybe if they left them alone down there in the dark until everything was prepared . . . Nils could stay up here and help fix the party.

Down in their dark room, the two culprits were not being as sorry for their misdoing as they might have been —at least Em was not. Em said they would not take their overalls off in the cold; they would wear them until the bed was warm. They took off their muddy shoes and crawled in under the covers. Their overalls were muddy too, but they would dry after a while when it got warm. And Em did not care that he was getting his bed dirty.

Then Em had another idea—he was a great boy for ideas. They were arguing about what was in Pegasus's rumble seat. Dwi thought he had seen onions by the flashlight when they came past. "No, it was apples," Em corrected him. "Let's go up and see." He was out of bed again in a jiffy.

"Don't, Em!" said Dwi. "Bea *will* spank you if you take an apple."

"All right, Dwi. I promise not to touch, only look."

In muddy shoes, with laces trailing after them, the two little boys scurried out into the snowstorm. They could see Bea and Lena and Nils, going back and forth and in and out, carrying apples in netting bags, carrots and onions, boxes with big bows, boxes with bottles in them.

Then the kitchen door shut, and everything was dark again. Only out of the kitchen window, over the roof of their own house, shone a light that looked very festive on such a night.

"That stinker!" Em said angrily.

"Who?" asked Dwi.

"Nils! He ate something, and he ought to come down too. I am going up on the roof to look in the window."

"Oh, Em, it's dangerous with all that snow and ice— and Lena could see you."

But Em was not to be stopped. And, as always, Dwi followed him, just like a little bird after a cuckoo. They went up the stairs to the top of their house and tiptoed

over the roof to the kitchen window. Then the door
opened and they threw themselves down flat in the snow.

"Someone there?" Lena asked. They could see Lena's
head in the doorway and Bea's in the window. They
waited, as quiet as two mice, with the snow whirling and
the wind howling round their icy ears. The door was
closed, the window-shade pulled down.

What the boys wanted now was to get back to their
beds and get warm. Like snakes they slid off the roof into

the mud; then they slithered down the stairs into their caboose and shut their door very, very carefully.

"I guess this time we'd better take our overalls off before we get into bed. They're sticky with mud," Em said philosophically.

As they were shedding their dirty clothes, they heard footsteps. They pushed their overalls under the bed and were in under the covers in a wink. They didn't think about the beds being cold now, and there was no time to put on pajamas. They closed their eyes, leaving only a crack open so they could see who was coming. Here came Lena, good angel, with a lantern and bathrobes.

"Come on, boys. Bea is not angry any more. She wants you to have nice hot baths."

Em sat up in bed. "Oh, my red cow, how I'd like a hot bath!" He grinned, although his teeth were chattering with cold.

Dwi jumped up and hugged Lena. "Oh, Lena, I love you. Will you carry me?"

"Why didn't you put on your pajamas this cold night?" Lena asked.

"Well, we couldn't see," explained Em. Lena took the pajamas from under the boys' pillows, and one, two, three, they were into them and the bathrobes.

When they reached the kitchen it was so stormy that the wind and snow blew them right in through the door. Being inside was almost too good to be true. The whole place smelled of beefsteak and onions and coffee. A big salad bowl was all ready with garlic and oil and potatoes and tomatoes and peppers. Nils was carrying a bowl of flowers to the big red table.

Em and Dwi tried to see everything at once, but Lena whisked them into the bathroom in a great rush. "How dirty you boys are!" she said. "My goodness, where have you been?"

"We—we—" Dwight began stammering.

Em took over. "Yes, we fell on the stairs, it was so slippery. And we had to crawl down."

Lena gave them a good soaking and a good soaping. They were very clean, pink-looking boys when they got to the living room.

It was really a party, with candles and flowers and a good big chunk of pitchwood burning in the fireplace. The beefsteak was eaten, and then came ice cream and the cake with nine candles. There were presents for everybody when Bea had a birthday. It was really a happy little little family.

9. Always Something Going On

Most of the days and weeks raced by like wildfire, and Nils had fun with Em and Dwi and was quite happy at the Rancho Arroyo. But now and again there came a spell when every hour seemed as long as a day and he was homesick and lonely. Then Nils would worry because

Mother and Bix were so long getting to America. He would have nightmares about dangerous things happening to them and wake up afraid that the little Hansen family was never going to be together again as it had been in Denmark. After such a dream he was no good at games with the other boys and just wandered around moodily by himself.

"What's the matter with Nils?" Em would ask Bea.

"Let him alone," Bea would say. "He will be all right soon." But she would talk to Nils herself about his family and about Denmark and the sea and all the little islands that he loved. Em and Dwi didn't know what it was like to be an island boy, to feel like a seagull lost in the mountains, but Bea seemed to guess.

"Aren't there any islands in America?" Nils asked once. "Not big islands, but little ones like Taosinge where we used to live in summer?"

So Bea told him about Maine, where she had spent a summer once, and the tiny green islands that sat like emeralds in the blue sea there. Nils thought that was where the Hansens ought to have their new home when they were all together again. "Is Maine near California?" he wanted to know, already full of plans.

But Bea got out her old school geography to show him

Maine on a map, and it was as far from California as one could get and still be in America. Nils sighed. It was going to be a lot more difficult to get there, then, but he wrote about Maine in a letter to his father anyway. And he told Mother and Bix about Maine too.

Saturday was always painting day for the boys. Nils made a great big picture for them with so many things in it that it was a real game to name them all. Sometimes they pretended they were living inside that picture and had all sorts of adventures there. It had the sea in it, of course, and this was the first time in their lives that Em and Dwi played in sand that smelled salty and found shells of different colors and learned what barnacles looked like.

At the Rancho Arroyo they had plenty of sand that was not salty—too much of it sometimes. They were playing in the big piano box when Nils saw his first sandstorm.

The piano box was big enough so that all three of them could take sunbaths in it at once. They wanted to get as brown as Indians, but it was February, and the wind was strong. They made little paper windmills, but the wind seemed to come from every direction, and sand began blowing into their eyes. Over back of the Black Mesa, the air and sky looked yellow because there was a gigantic sandstorm blowing up there. By the time the boys got indoors it had reached the Rancho Arroyo.

How it blew! The sand beat against the little houses and crept in under the doors and on the windowsills. It stung their faces when they had to go out to do their chores. You couldn't get away from it. Sarco and Patches were in their barn, but the poor cows and horses out on the Indian land stood with their heads down and tried to turn their tails to the wind that kept swirling round them.

After a while the sandstorm made the boys nervous. They were restless and naughty, but this time they were not punished. Bea and Lena played games with them, with prizes for the winners and gifts for everybody, and it turned out to be a good party after all.

For a whole month it was dry and windy. In church the priest prayed for rain. The Indians danced their rain dance. Then one day, as the forty children streamed out of school, Nils saw the government rainmaker. Over the Jemez Mountains big cumulus clouds stood quietly, and the plane circled them. Then it flew right into one.

"What is he doing?" Nils asked.

"He is seeding the clouds with dry ice," someone said. "No, it is silver iodide," said another.

However it was done, certainly something was happening up there. Suddenly the clouds were bulking up in the air just like boiling porridge—higher and higher—and larger and larger.

Pegasus pulled up in the schoolyard. "Hurry," called Bea. "We want to get back before the thunderstorm is over us. Come on, all of you, pile in front here."

It grew dark as Pegasus rumbled off toward home. It thundered over the Jemez Mountains, then over the Sangre de Cristo Mountains. While they were driving along the dry river bed it started to hail.

"Ouch!" cried Em.

"That hurts!" said little Dwi.

"*Av for Soren!*" said Nils. He got a big piece of ice smack in one eye. Another scraped his cheek.

"Let's get the top up, boys! Quick, now!"

Old Pegasus had a canvas top. They got it up, one boy struggling on each side, and Bea in the middle. The old friend was now nice and cozy inside—if only the windows had not been torn out. But it was a lot better, anyway, and off they went in the hailstorm. Cows jumped from the river bed up into the chamiso bushes, and wild little Indian horses galloped in front of the car. Thunder roared, and it had grown so black that streaks of lightning fairly blinded everybody. And it rained. How it rained!

Bea had to cross the river. The car went all right along the old path, but soon there was so much water they had to make a detour. Then Pegasus balked as water came rushing down. Bea looked serious, but she tried again. The old car lurched, sling-slang from left to right, went

down into a hole, and came up again. The water sprayed
out from the wheels so that Pegasus looked like a ship
cutting through waves. Nils gave a yelp.

"Don't scream in a car!" scolded Bea. It was the first
time she had been cross with Nils, so he knew she was
worried. She gave the old car a little more gas; it choked
and stopped. "Oh, dear," said Bea, "now the carburetor
is flooded." They had to wait a few minutes, with water
swirling round them. At last Bea took a deep breath and
tried once more. The car jumped out of the hole and
rumbled up the path in the stream; it picked up speed,
dashed up the steep river bank and onto the road. They
were all wet, but Bea laughed with relief. "Good old
Pegasus," she said, patting the wheel.

When they passed the postbox, Bea opened it without
getting out of the car. Letters and magazines and packages were stuffed into the mailbag in a hurry. They
rounded the corner by Señor Pedro's place and up their
own arroyo to the rancho.

It rained. It poured. It seemed as if it was never going
to stop raining. Everything was sticky and wet. Even
sketchboxes and paintboxes were soaking.

"Is it really those government rainmakers who make
all this mess?" Nils asked.

"Who knows?" said Bea. "The Indians have danced the rain dance for a month. Maybe it's the Indians. Father Antonio prayed for rain last Sunday. Maybe it's Father Antonio's rain. Anyway, we need it."

Soon everybody was dry and reading letters. There was one for Em and Dwi from their father, and another for Bea. Lena had one, but she got through reading it very quickly; it was just a bill for her new hat. There were two letters for Nils, both of them short but exciting. Mother wrote from Copenhagen: she had sold the house and had got a passport for herself and Bix. Now all she needed was the permit to get into the United States. And Father wrote that it would not be long before Mr. Mitchell from San Bernardino would come to take Nils to California.

Em and Dwi taught Nils the catalogue game that afternoon. The enormous Sears Roebuck catalogue had hundreds and hundreds of pages, and on every page there were dozens of pictures of things for sale. The game was to shut your eyes, open the catalogue to a page, and put your finger down. Then you opened your eyes to see what you had got. When little Dwi got an English bicycle with three gears he was so happy he threw himself down on the floor.

"Now it's my turn," said Em. He got a pair of blue jeans—man's size. "Oh, I'll try again," he said.

Dwi sat up. "No, Em, you're cheating. It's Nils' turn now."

Nils put his finger on a toy ship. It was a little steamer. "Oh, that's for his mother to come in," said Dwi. "That is a lucky sign."

They played again, and went on playing until they began to hear some funny little noises—*plink! plink! plonk!*

Bea saw that water was dripping down on the chimney shelves. She spread out newspaper, and the drops came more quickly—*spit, spat, spat!* Outside there was a regular cloudburst, and the thunder and lightning had come back again.

"Oh, dear," said Bea, "I'll have to get Hilario to spread crank-case oil on the roofs. Lena!" she called. "Please look in the bedrooms. It's dripping in here."

Lena came in from the kitchen, where she had been cleaning carrots. "Oh, my! Dripping so soon!" She hurried into the bedroom. The green silk cover on Bea's bed already had a puddle in the middle. Lena emptied the muddy water onto the floor and pushed the bed away from the drip. On her way to the kitchen for a bowl, she peeped into the guest room. Mud was running down the white wall back of the bed. She moved that bed, too, and an oil painting of flowers.

More drips—more bowls! More drips—and pots and pans and even saucers, anything they could find to hold water.

Nils didn't like the thunderclaps, but he put on a brave face and raced down the stairs to the boys' room. He was back soon, reporting that everything was wet but he had moved all their beds.

How Lena and Bea worked! They rolled up rugs and changed everything from one place to another until the house looked worse than it would have on moving day or in an earthquake. Bea's best crystal bowl was put in the middle of the floor; a huge glop of mud fell plunk into it with a splash like a fountain. There was nothing to do but try to find themselves some dry places.

They ate their dinner at the red table as usual, but to the music of *bing-bung! plink-a! ping! pong! ging! gang!* PLONK! Every pot and bowl had its own little tune. At last it sounded so ridiculous that they were all laughing their heads off. They went to bed to the song of *plong-plong-plong!*

Even after the rain stopped the boys had to stay home from school because they could never have got through the river bed, which wasn't a dry arroyo any longer. But there was plenty of work for everybody. Em and Dwi brought in the wood and fed the animals. Nils emptied all the pots and washed them clean. Lena washed the furniture and the walls and the doors and the floors and the windows. Bea went off to bring Hilario to fix the roof.

By the time Hilario arrived the boys had crackling fires burning in all the stoves and fireplaces to dry out the house. Hilario was a very good friend. He came with a wagon and two horses, and he wore his tropical helmet and white work gloves. He had everything with him for waterproofing a roof made of clay, and four cans of heavy crank-case oil to spread over the clay, and a load of long willow branches.

They could not have done without Hilario on the rancho. He helped with the garden and kept fences in repair. He sawed down trees and brought pitchwood from the mountains.

Now he had to work all that day and the next day. There were still big angry clouds round the mountain valleys. The rivers were swollen and angry. But here over the little Rancho Arroyo the sun shone hot. The roof dried and got hard as a brick again.

Hilario made interesting things. He mixed clay and small pieces of straw, poured it into boxes and dried a whole row of boxes in the sun. This was to repair the wall steps and the stairs down to the boys' house.

Of course the boys had to play with the mud, too. They filled all the small boxes in the house with straw and clay and put them out to dry; Hilario could use those. Then they started making birds and pots and horses—even pigs with holes in their backs to put nickels in.

"It is good to have a savings bank," said Nils. "We will paint them."

"I know," said Em, who always knew everything. "The Indians use clay that the color never comes off. It is black and yellow and red, with some blue. Come on, I know where we can get some."

They hurried down the road over the cattle-guard. At Señor Pedro's farm they found the big white horse whinnying to her colt. The colt was outside the fence, and the two animals could not figure out how to get together. Only the little girl in the red dress was home, but she came as quick as a mouse when the boys told her what had happened. Together she and the three boys got the colt back inside the corral with its mother.

By now Em and Dwi had forgotten about the clay, but

Nils reminded them. They ran down along the river bed to where some Indians were digging their pottery clay. They could not get much, because water was still rushing down from the mountains, but they brought back enough to make a long row of animals and pots. Bea told them that she had some colored lacquers and some shellac they could use when the clay dried.

Easter came, and there had to be something extra beside the usual Sunday treat, which was Danish pastry with their morning milk. Nils had found out that they called the pastries "butterhorns" in America, and they were very good too.

While the boys were out Bea and Lena made up three baskets of colored paper, each with sugar eggs and two real eggs, painted, and each with tiny yellow cotton chickens perched on top.

The baskets were under the beds on Easter morning. Em and Dwi knew what to expect. As soon as they opened their eyes they turned over, bottoms up, to fish underneath for the treasure. Nils waked to see two bottoms in striped pajama pants up in the air. It was a funny way to sleep, he thought. Then two tousled heads appeared, and hands holding pretty baskets.

"Hey, dive, Nils!" Em laughed. Nils dived. And up he came with a beautiful Easter basket!

Em was in a hurry. He scrambled into his clothes. "Come on, Nils, we have to go out and hunt eggs!" What a remarkable place—to have more eggs hidden after they had the baskets already!

Out the boys rushed—Dwi still in his bathrobe, Em put together any old way, and Nils tripping over his shoe-laces. The Easter rabbit had hidden eggs everywhere for them. There were tiny birds' nests with two eggs in each. There were eggs painted with faces—Dwi's face, Em's face, Nils' face! A lot of others had funny faces painted on them.

10. Three Boys in a Rumble Seat

The snow was melting in the mountains. The water roared and raced and crashed down, carrying trees and boulders along the river beds. Around corners, around mountains, around forests it came, and nobody could stop it. The water rushed down the Pojoaque Valley, down to Nambe and the other little Spanish villages. It ran and ran. It made big walls break. Large rocks tumbled along and filled the river beds that were the arroyo roads over which boys went to school. Cars going to Santa Fe stuck fast in mud. Trucks pulled them out—then the trucks got stuck. Nils saw one car that had sunk until only its roof showed—and it wasn't even raining.

Nils remembered the big dams his father worked on, and he tried to explain to Em and Dwi how they could dam up all this water and save it for when it was needed for crops in dry weather. He wasn't clear just how it was to be done, but he thought they ought to begin with a dike.

"Let's go down to the river and make a dike," said Em. They started off.

"Have you done your chores, boys?" Bea called after them.

"Yes, a long time ago."

"Has Sarco got water?"

"We're taking him down to the river now," said Em quickly.

But Bea had another idea. They could water Sarco right in his barn and then get their tools to fix up the dry arroyo. So they all went down to the one river bed that had already dried out and worked like grownup men. Em had already done this several times in his young life, and even little Dwi remembered last year. They made a new road in the gravel so they could get from their farm to the driveway the other cars had already made in the river bed. It was a big job for three small boys, and Bea was very pleased with them.

"I am going to try the new road with Pegasus," she told them. "We have to go to Santa Fe to do the marketing—we're out of all kinds of supplies. You boys can come along. All three of you ride in the rumble seat, and Lena will sit in front with me."

That was a surprise. Em and Dwi knew they would get ice-cream cones at the drugstore, and each of them had fifteen cents to buy things at the five-and-ten. But Nils, who had never seen Santa Fe, was even more excited.

They were sent to wash up and put on clean clothes. They left their room a mess, but they came out so scrubbed and combed you would hardly have recognized them. Em was wearing brown corduroy overalls and a blue blouse; Dwi, blue overalls and a purple blouse. And Nils wore his very best sailor suit.

"Bea," Em said, "the next time we get clothes, I want a sailor suit just like Nils'."

Bea looked at him. "Nils, you are really too elegant to

ride in the rumble seat with that suit. You must sit in front with us."

Nils' eyes grew round and sad. And both Bea and Lena understood very well that it was more fun to sit in the rumble seat with two other boys than up in front between an aunt and a helper. So kind Lena found a pair of overalls that would fit him, and one, two, three—Nils was changed into an American boy.

Sarco looked after them over the half-door of the barn. From the top of the house Silver seriously watched their departure. He knew that when they went away it was his job to take care of the rancho, where not a single door was ever locked, day or night. He looked very important, and he was. He would guard the house and chase strange horses and cows out of the alfalfa. "Good boy!" Bea and the boys called to Silver as they left.

Trusty paid no attention to any of them. He was lying flat as a pancake. Only his head was up as he watched for the bluebirds that had come back for the spring.

Brump! Bang! Brrr! Around the well and down the hill old Pegasus went. Across the cattle-guard and along the new driveway and out into the river bed, the dry one, they went. They did not go the usual way because the

San Ildefonso road was closed, with the Nambe River still behaving as roughly as a team of wild horses. So they took the dry arroyo straight up hill into the Indian land, up and down, in and out. Where they met the big yellow road scraper they had to turn off and wait.

"What is that?" asked Nils, pointing to a lot of bones and a big white skull.

"Oh, that's the skeleton of a cow that drowned here last year in a flood," Em told him.

"Do you have floods too?"

"Oh, yes," said Em, "but only in summer. There is a special place in the mountains where, if there is a cloud-burst, the water rushes down in this arroyo so fast that cows and horses sometimes can't get away fast enough. You don't have to worry, though; the cloudbursts won't come now—not until May or June."

Bumpety-bump! "Hold on, boys," Bea called, "now we are in the wash."

Pegasus jumped along like an old race horse, past a house where a fat old watchdog lumbered into the road to bark after them. Then the car scrambled and slithered down a hillside and landed on its nose in the river.

"Oh!" screamed Nils.

The other two boys were laughing.

Bea called, "Nils, you must not scream in a car. It disturbs the driver, you know. Nothing bad is going to happen; this is not dangerous."

"All right," said Nils. "I'll never scream any more." He felt ashamed of himself.

Splash—splush—squuush, sli-i-ip! The car was stuck in the water. Bea tried to back up; she tried to go ahead. But old Pegasus was helpless, with front wheels in mud to the axle and rear wheels in quicksand. Now Nils thought it was fun; the other boys squealed with joy.

It began to rain a little. That made the bank muddier and slipperier than ever. Two horses came along, pulling a wagonload of wood. The driver tried to pull Pegasus out with a chain. But the horses were skinny and his wagon was heavy, and they couldn't do it. Bea went off, riding with the farmer, to get help. The others sat in the car, axle-deep in water.

Then Lena had an idea. "Take off your shoes and socks, boys, and we'll try to turn the stream with these big pine branches."

In a minute the boys were out of the rumble seat with their overalls rolled up high. That was fun as well as work. They took enormous pine branches from a pile left beside the river for that purpose and dragged them along the road where the river was rushing, trying to change the course of the stream. It was a fine idea, but it did not work.

Then came the big yellow truck from San Ildefonso, filled with yellow signs to post along the road: DANGEROUS, DETOUR, and so forth. It stopped, and the men piled out of the truck without any questions. They stretched a big chain from the truck to the car and started tugging. For a while it looked as if Pegasus were just being stretched out, longer and longer, until he would snap in two. But suddenly he popped out of the mud like a cork out of a bottle of champagne.

"Hooray!" shouted the boys, and Lena thanked the three nice, smiling young men. Nils thought it would be a good job to be a road man and put signs in dangerous places to warn people, and help people out of the mud. He wished his father were here; *he* could tell them what to do to keep the water away from the road.

Lena started the car, and off they went, to find Bea inside a little store, drying her clothes and phoning to get help. The sun was shining again.

It was a beautiful trip along the Santa Fe Trail. Indians with horses and plows were smoothing the hillside down to the highway. They were sowing grass seed and planting little trees. The Indians looked beautiful to Nils, with red handkerchiefs around their black hair. Their horses were small and stiff-necked. The near hills were rose-colored and the mountains purple and blue. The clouds were soft and white now, with sun-gilded edges, and the three boys in the rumble seat watched them, picking out the different shapes—a horse and rider, a dog sitting up on his hind legs, a camel, an old man with a very big beard.

They passed the Tesuque Indian Pueblo but had no time to stop and see it. On the road an Indian stood, with a turquoise handkerchief round his hair, which hung in two long braids with turquoise yarn plaited into them. Over his shoulder he wore a blanket of many colors. Nils nearly fell out of the car to look. The Indian held up his right hand to show them that he wanted a ride to Santa Fe.

"Oh, let's stop!" said Nils.

"There's no room for him, Nils," Em said. "Bea always picks up Indians who ask for a ride if she has room in the car. We almost always have one when we go from Santa Fe to Tesuque."

Nils thought it was bad there was no room today. He would have liked to look at the Indian close up and for

a long time. But the boys told him he would see lots of Indians in Santa Fe.

"Really?" Nils could hardly believe there would be lots of them.

"Yes, at Dick's shop. You know, he's an Indian trader and he has all kinds of things from the Indian pueblos."

"I am going to be an Indian trader," said Dwi.

"What's an Indian trader?" Nils asked. Really he was ashamed that Dwi, a little boy only half his size, should know when he didn't.

"Don't you know what a trader is?" Dwi asked. "Well, it's a—it's a man who has a desk and a lot of bows and arrows and drums."

"Dwi doesn't know," Em told Nils. "But I do. A trader is a man who exchanges things with Indians. If the Indians want something they can get at Dick's they give him silver things or rugs or pottery for it, never money."

The car was running along the top of the world. They could see all of Santa Fe down in a valley. Think of it—down in a valley! And Bea had told Nils that Santa Fe was up in the Sangre de Cristo Mountains, seven thousand feet higher than the ocean. The rancho in Pojoaque was six thousand feet high.

In a few minutes Pegasus was running along a beautiful avenue in a whole row of cars. It looked as if every American who went to Santa Fe must have a car. There were big stores on both sides of the street. Bea let the boys go with her into the big market. Em and Dwi were arguing about whose turn it was to push the shop car. Nils had no idea what a shop car was, but this time he didn't ask; he waited to see.

"Nils can help me," said Bea, "while Em and Dwi look at things."

Lena went to the library while Bea and the boys went marketing. Inside the store Nils saw not one long counter, as they had in shops where he came from, but seven little counters with cash registers, and fourteen big boys working at them. Nils had no time to see what they were doing because they were through a little gate and Bea thrust the handle of a shop car into his hand. It was a cart on rubber-tired wheels, with one wire basket on top and another underneath.

Nils pushed the little wagon and followed Bea, who began putting things into the baskets. He had never seen such a store. There were long aisles like streets—Tin Can Street, Soap Street, Cracker Street, Fruit Street, and many more. Wagon after wagon went down these aisles, and people just took things off shelves to put in their baskets. Nils had never seen the like.

Em and Dwi came along, and when Nils talked to them he found that Bea had disappeared down Coffee Street to Cake Street, then up Meat Street to Butter Street. He had lost her, and she had taken the shop car with her. "We'll find her when she comes to pay," Em said.

So the three boys took a tour through the whole place. They looked at pictures on boxes—raisins and macaroni, and a colored lady with a whole plate of pancakes. Mushrooms and grapejuice and chicken soup—nothing was put away in drawers at all. Everything was neatly packaged in cans or boxes or cellophane bags, ready to take off the shelves. Only the vegetables and fresh fruit had to be packed. The vegetables looked very beautiful under a fine spray of water that kept them green and shiny. There were scales so people could weigh them up for themselves. The potatoes were in red net bags.

The boys finally spotted Bea's red hat far away by the exit and hurried after her. The car she had piled up was a fine sight—oranges and grapefruit and grapes and eggplant, squash and celery and a bag of potatoes, lots of tin cans with pictures on them, and sacks of macaroni and cookies and nuts and even candies; pears and strawberries and flour in snow-white sacks, chocolate and tomatoes and apples. It looked as if they would never have to shop again, but Bea knew that all this wouldn't last her family more than a week.

The entrance to one of the seven counters where she went in looked to Nils like the gate to Tivoli, the amusement park in Copenhagen. The boy worked with one hand taking things out of the basket, the other going *cli-clap, cli-clap* on the adding machine. The second boy stood at the end of the counter, putting all the things that had been counted into big paper sacks with handles while Bea paid some dollars. This was really business, Nils decided, and he thought he would like to build such a market in his home town of Holte.

On their way to the five-and-ten-cent store Nils saw an Indian standing on a corner with a handful of things to sell. "Hello, Ahkelano," Bea said to him. "How is your little boy?"

Ahkelano smiled and shook hands with Bea and with the boys.

"This is Nils," said Bea. "Nils is from Denmark."

Nils was very excited to be shaking hands with a real Indian. "Do you sell things, Ahkelano?" he asked in a shaking voice.

"Yes, Nils, you want to buy?" Ahkelano showed very white teeth in a smile.

"Yes. Bea, can I? These little dolls?"

"That is rain god," said Ahkelano.

Nils counted out his twenty-five cents and took the little doll. He had traded with a real live Indian. He was as happy as a blackbird with a worm. That little god would be his mascot, his lucky piece, and nobody would ever get it away from him. It was painted all sorts of colors and had tiny feathers on its head.

"Katchina!" said Ahkelano. Nils looked at him stupidly.

"Ahkelano is telling you that the Indians call their rain gods Katchina," Bea explained.

"I have to see Dick," Ahkelano told Bea. "I meet Eaglefeather there in ten minutes." Ahkelano was from Santo Domingo, and he wore a red velvet blouse and a heavy silver necklace, and a silver belt and silver bracelets with blue stones. Nils wished he could earn enough money to buy a bracelet like that; and here he was so poor, he had not a cent left. In a shop window he saw another red velvet tunic, and lying on it was a most beautiful necklace with a lot of blue stones.

"Bea, how many dollars do you think that necklace would cost?" he asked.

"Oh, Nils, that one is worth a fortune—a hundred dollars, maybe. You see, it is a squash-blossom necklace. All around there are silver squash blossoms, and the medallion in the center is a symbol of the rain god."

"A hundred dollars is a lot of money," Nils said in a small voice. He looked at the squash-blossom necklace and sighed deeply. It would be better to give Mother something else. He would ask Dick about bows and arrows.

Em and Dwi had a busy time doing their trading at the five-and-ten-cent store, but Nils had already spent his money. He was satisfied with just looking at such a wonderful assortment of things on counters, and keeping a close hold on his rain doll. Then Bea saw to it that he got an ice-cream cone with the other boys, even if he didn't have any money.

"Now, boys," Bea said, "we will have a big day because we don't know when we will be coming to Santa Fe again. Let's pay Dick a visit."

Em and Dwi ran round a corner, and Nils followed them to where a sign said TRADING POST. They went into a little courtyard between two adobe walls, but the post wasn't open. There was a little white card on the door. "Coming Back at Once," Nils read.

Bea had met some people on the street she wanted to talk to, so the three boys sat on an adobe bench and waited for Dick to come back at once. But at once became rather a long time. "I guess he's out trading with the Indians," Em explained.

Two Indians came into the courtyard. One of them was carrying a lot of bows and arrows, and Nils jumped up, feeling as if he were in the middle of one of the books his father used to read to him—*The Pathfinder* or *The Last of the Mohicans.*

"Hello, Talano," Em said to an old Indian with turquoise ribbons wound round his hair and a very wide smile on his very wrinkled face.

"Hello, boys. Is Dick not home? This is Santiago from Santa Clara." Then the boys introduced Nils to Talano and Santiago. Even Em was impressed with meeting Santiago. "Uncle Dick says he is more than a hundred years old," he whispered to Nils.

The two Indians sat down on the bench with the boys to wait for Dick. Nils could hardly sit still, he was so excited.

Santiago had two long pieces of fur tied to his white hair. They interested Dwi, and he trotted over to be taken up on the ancient Indian's knee. "You are very old, aren't you, Santiago?" Dwi asked.

The old Indian grinned, and his eyes disappeared in wrinkles. "Yes," he said. "I don't know how old, but somebody said a hundred and two. I am very old all right."

Dwi stroked the fur tied to Santiago's braids. "What's that?"

"Beaver," said the Indian.

"Beaver? That's the animal that saws down trees, isn't it? Why do they do that?"

"You ask many questions," said Santiago. "The beaver saws trees down to make himself bridges and dams."

"What do they saw with?" Dwi asked.

"With their teeth," said the old Indian.

Em was talking with his old friend Talano. "Are you going to trade all these bows and arrows to Dick, Talano?"

Yes, Talano was going to trade with Dick.

Nils longed to get into the conversation with the Indians. He tried Santiago. "Do you have a house, sir?" he asked.

Santiago grinned so that Nils could see he had only two teeth left. He thought it was funny that Nils called him "sir," and he told the Danish boy that he had three names. "My Indian name is O-ye-ga-pai, my Spanish name is Santiago Naranjo, and my American name is Jim Orange. And I have a house in Santa Clara. You know Santa Clara?"

"No," Nils said. "Not yet, O-ye-ga-pai."

"Fine. How could you remember that hard Indian name, Nils?"

"Oh, I thought it was so beautiful! Are you going to trade with Dick too?"

"No," said Santiago O-ye-ga-pai. "I am governor— Indian chief. We are going to talk about some serious things."

Nils' eyes got bigger. "Are you making war?" he asked.

The Indian chief laughed. "Not making war—oh, no. Drawings! Do you know Indian drawings?"

"I have seen the rain gods," said Nils.

Santiago took an arrow from his friend Talano and made a drawing in the sand. "Look, Nils, this is the Santa Clara deer. This one is a rainbow drawing. Clouds here. This is a thunderbird."

Em and Dwi were just as interested as Nils now. Em sat with all of Talano's bows and arrows in his arms. Dwi held his drums.

"Here you see a San Ildefonso thunderbird." Talano made a very good drawing in the sand.

"Look, boys, the sun god." Santiago smiled.

The boys were so absorbed they forgot all about Bea and Dick. Now they were going to art school to these old fine Indian artists, the Santa Clara chief and the San Ildefonso Indian.

Suddenly Bea was there, looking down at the sand and seeing something more beautiful than a painting.

Talano saw her. "Hello, Bea. We have a good time here. Nice boys."

Bea looked at the boys with their arms full of bows and arrows and drums. She asked Talano if she could talk with him for a minute, and the two of them went out on the sidewalk. When they came back into the courtyard Dick was with them and they all went into his beautiful shadowy shop.

The boys looked at everything, but they thought that Talano's bows and arrows and drums were better than anything else there.

"Come along now," said Bea. "Dick must have a chance to talk business with Talano and O-ye-ga-pai."

The boys gave the bows and arrows back to Talano. "You take one—each of you," Talano said.

The boys looked at Bea. "Yes, you may take them. Say a nice thank-you to Talano."

Em and Dwi had taken their bows and arrows, smooth white cottonwood bows with Indian painting on them, and arrows with eagle feathers dyed red and yellow. Nils was not sure that he was to have one too. He was not an old friend of Talano's like the boys from the rancho.

"Nils," said Talano, "here!" He handed a beautiful big bow and two arrows to Nils. Nils' heart banged like a church bell at a wedding. He clicked his heels together and gave Talano his hand with his very best dancing-school bow, just as he had done it for the captain of the *Gripsholm* when he came to America.

"Thank you a lot, Talano. I will give you something

too." From his pocket he pulled out some loose buttons, very favorite ones that he had changed over from the pocket of his sailor suit. Two buttons had crowns on them and were from the uniform of the King's Guard, one from a Danish postman's uniform had a trumpet on it, and one that had once been worn by a Danish policeman had an eye in the middle.

"You are a good friend, Nils," said Talano. "I like these. Are they from your country?"

Nils explained the uniform buttons, and Talano was very glad to have them. "I will show them to the medicine man at San Ildefonso. I like that one with the eye."

Two other tall Indians came in, Navahos with red and blue velvet blouses and a lot of silver jewelry. The last thing Nils saw as the boys and Bea went away was all the Indians looking with interest at his buttons.

In his hand he carried a real Indian bow and Indian arrows! His bow was even bigger than the bows Em and Dwi had. Nobody could measure the pride Nils felt inside his chest.

Bea and the boys walked down the street toward an enormous adobe castle that Bea said was the Hotel La Fonda. And there, getting out of her car, was Margaret. Nils thought she looked like one of the gilded and painted angels in the little Danish church at Turö. It was a very gay angel, however, who called out to them, "Hello, I'm treating you to tea. Let's go in."

Just then a very big, dusty bus rolled up in front of the hotel. Nils heard that it was a Greyhound; and indeed there was a greyhound painted on the side of it, bounding along as if he were racing the bus. Em said you could go all over America in a Greyhound bus, from New York to California, and always traveling very fast, eighty miles an hour. Bea had told Em and Dwi about Greyhounds, how the big chairs inside could be made into beds at night, and how there was air-conditioning.

"What is air-conditioning?" the Danish boy asked. But when it came to explaining it, neither Em nor Dwi knew precisely what air-conditioning was either. "Come on," Em said quickly, "Margaret's giving a party."

So they went into the adobe castle, into a hall that looked to Nils as big as a whole town. There were carved wooden columns and carved beams in the high ceiling. The Mexican tin lanterns on the whitewashed walls were painted green and red, and there were oil paintings of the beautiful New Mexico mountains. Best of all, there was a portrait of an Indian, painted with all the feathers Nils had seen in his book at home in Denmark. It was

Santiago! Nils stood there so still and so long that the others had to call him three times to come along.

Nils thought the people in the hotel were as remark-able as the adobe castle itself. Indians were there, and cowboys with immense ten-gallon hats and embroidered boots; ladies wearing narrow blue trousers and red blouses like the Indians, with huge silver belts and necklaces. Such people really belonged in story books.

Down the long hall they went, and Nils stopped in front of an Indian and Mexican art shop full of the most fantastic things—pottery and silver and dolls, Indian costumes and masks. Bea and the others had gone on, and Nils had to hurry to catch up, down a long passage where garlands of chilas and cornhusks hung on the walls.

In the room where the tea was served there was a fireplace from floor to ceiling with blazing logs as big as a whole man. Everything was bigger in America, even the black Spanish table that held dozens of plates of cookies and cakes! The tablecloth was fire red, and so were the curtains, and the chairs were red leather. Nils looked and looked so he would remember all this to tell Mother in his next letter.

A girl with black, black eyes smiled at Nils and gave him a fire-red napkin and a plate of little red and blue and green cookies. Her black skirt that went right down to the floor had lots of colored ribbons sewed round it, and it went *swish-swish* when she walked. Another girl,

as beautiful as the first and dressed like her, brought a cake that had been under a big cover on the table. There were fine little sandwiches and tea with sugar and orange.

Some men came in with clothes as fancy as those the girls wore—red silk blouses and red sashes and black trousers slit up the side like the ones in pictures of toreadors Nils had seen. He was alarmed. He hoped they were not going to have a bullfight, because that he did *not* want to look at. But it was all right; they were musicians and began to play very gay, peppy Spanish music. Nils felt his feet jigging as he sat in his chair, and the grown-ups left their places to dance, just as Nils had danced folk dances at home.

The most beautiful of the Spanish girls came over to Nils and said, "Come, we will dance too." She was lovely, with her hair parted in the middle and drawn smoothly back, just the way Mother wore hers, though Mother's was yellow and this girl's hair was black as a raven's wing. She had a red flower in her hair, and her eyes looked as if they were edged with black ribbons, just like little Bix's Sunday coat.

Nils did want to dance. "But what about my bow and arrows?" he asked.

Margaret promised to hold his bow and arrows, so Nils danced to the music that got right into his toes. All the people were laughing and dancing now, and some of them were singing. Em was playing a violin in the air, using his bow and arrow, and Dwi danced with Bea. Tra-la-*la*-la, tra-la-*la*-la, tra-la-*la*-la-la, *la!* went the music and Nils' heart.

At last Bea said it was snowing again and they would have to hurry to get home. It was already dark and quite cold when the three boys clambered into the rumble seat again, in among celery and oranges and lots of tin cans. They each had a blanket and, just like Eskimo dogs, they made themselves three holes to go to bed in. Snowflakes spittered in on them now and again, but they were nice and cozy and they talked about their big day. So many things had happened, it was really more like three days.

When at last they heard the river again—*sss-sss*—Bea was very careful. Three faces peered out of the rumble seat, trying to see the muddy stream with its big waves in the dark. The boys got water in their faces from the cascades the wheels threw up, but Bea got through all right this time.

Hoopla—they were up over the river bank on the other side! Bumpety bump, they went round a corner and across a bridge over the irrigation ditch, with all the loose boards rattling and jumping as they hit them. Soon they were home.

Not very much talk was heard that night in the boys' room.

11. Good-by to New Mexico

It was time to plant the garden and to get the alfalfa watered. Bea had brought seeds—beans, peas, squash, lots of vegetables; flower seeds too, such as California poppies.

The earth was hard as rock, and they had to break it with a pick to get it ready for the seeds. Though he was only seven years old, Em was very strong—and he liked showing off just how strong he was! "I can do it," he always said; and he did do it until Bea told him to stop before he hurt his back. Fat little Dwi sat on his heels watching—he always had an easy way to help. Bea was working in pigskin gloves.

Nils thought the way of planting here was very

peculiar and not right. Now in Denmark they did it so.
. . . He started to sow his poppy seeds in the ground
with no gloves on. When he had worked only a little he
found that his fingers were full of cactus pins. "It hurts,"
he said, sucking at them.

Bea grinned at him. "Do as I do, Nils. Here in the
desert we are different. You don't have cactus in Denmark, as we have. And you have rain in summer, but
we don't."

"Oh," said Nils.

"You see, Nils, that's why we build up these small
hills for the beans, and long small mountain ranges for
the other vegetables, because we water them from the
ditches. The water runs from there, and we lead it into
these smaller ditches so it can stay for a few days like
little canals."

Nils understood now how it was different—different
earth, different climate. It made him feel very far from
Denmark.

The garden was finished. It had to be, because tomorrow was "Bea's water day." Nils was to learn what that
meant.

At five o'clock next morning Hilario arrived with six
men. They burned the tumbleweed and the wild, dry

things in the deep-water irrigation ditch on top of the hill. They burned and cleaned.

The boys were there with them the whole day. Bea had to send out a pail of summer drinks to the men. Lena poured the drinks and said funny things that kept the men in a fine humor. And they worked so hard that they had to have two more pails and more fun with Lena.

The boys were dirty from head to foot by the time the irrigation channel was clean in the afternoon. The different "water porches" to the fields were closed tight. The gate from the river was opened, and in roared the water with a mighty swoosh.

Hilario opened Bea's gate, and into all the small canals ran glistening streams like silver serpents. Then the gate that led to a waterfall was opened wider, and the water was directed down over the hillside into the alfalfa field. Em and Bea and Nils were down there with spades to lead the water over the whole field. Little Dwi jumped around in the mud with his own little spade to "help."

It took three hours, and the boys thought it was a wonderful job. But Bea was glad to get it over. The gate was closed, and the boys got a big tub of water to wash themselves and their overalls and their rubber boots. There was a lot of fun around that tub until Bea called, "Emerson! Do you want to go after the mail?"

Oh, my, those boys were tired suddenly! They had sore feet and no dry shoes.

Bea and Lena said something in the kitchen. Then Lena said, "Never mind, I can pick up the mail when I go by with Pegasus. I am going to the movies."

"What!" all three boys screamed. "To the *movies?* May we go along?"

Bea laughed. "What about being so tired, and those sore feet and wet shoes?"

"Oh, Bea, you could let us go," Em coaxed. "Nils has *never* seen a movie here."

"Please, Lena," said Dwi. "Dear Lena, I love you."

Nils didn't say a word. He couldn't believe it. They wouldn't let old tired Pegasus run forty miles just to take them to a movie, would they?

"Shoes on in a hurry, then," Lena said. She was getting out her hat. In a very few minutes the boys were in clean overalls and Pegasus went *fut-a-da-fut* over the cattle-guard. On the way the boys picked pictures out of the clouds again and sang songs.

"It ain't gonna rain no mo', no mo',
It ain't gonna rain no mo'—
But how in the world can the old folks tell
That it ain't gonna rain no mo'?"

Nils saw a huge piece of pink quartz with a whole book of mica sticking out of it, and Lena stopped Pegasus so he could get it.

All four of them enjoyed a good old Western film with lots of horses in it, and lots of shooting. Afterward they had ice-cream cones and Dwi said, "Bang! Bang!" in the car until he feel asleep.

The vegetables were soon growing, and the California poppies came up. The neighbors had all had their different water days, and the boys had helped everywhere. After Nils had a letter from Father, telling him that Mr. Mitchell would come in another week to take him to California, the days raced by like the quickest of wildfire. Suddenly Bea seemed like a very wonderful aunt. New Mexico was a wonderful country and the Rancho Arroyo was a wonderful farm. Em and Dwi were wonderful, so were Silver and Trusty, and Sarco and Patches. It would be hard to leave them all.

Saying good-by was just as hard as Nils had thought it would be. He sat in Mr. Mitchell's car and waved. The boys waved and waved, and Bea and Lena wiped their eyes. Nils kept on waving even after they were across the cattle-guard.

Mr. Mitchell was a kind man. He looked a little bit like Nils' father, but he was shorter and broader. He had gray, smiling eyes. Afterward Nils didn't remember so very much about the trip to California. He grew very tired of riding in the car, and it was so hot when they drove through the valleys that it made him very sleepy and headachy.

San Bernardino was better because Mrs. Mitchell was kind and saw that he got a nice cool bath and a good rest. Mr. Mitchell was an orange-grower, and he took Nils to show him the groves of orange trees—one after another in long rows. Nils saw fan palms and date palms and palms that looked as if they were wearing coats. He saw pepper trees all red with pepper berries, and camphor trees and eucalyptus trees that looked ragged and smelled very good.

But the oranges were the best of all. "You can pick yourself all you want," Mr. Mitchell told Nils. "They're just fine now in April."

Very excited, Nils picked some big ones. "You know, Mr. Mitchell," he said, "when we get oranges in Denmark they have the name Sunkist written on them. Isn't that a beautiful name?"

Mr. Mitchell laughed and sounded very pleased. "Those oranges come from here, Nils. These are Sunkist oranges."

Nils thought that was the most remarkable coincidence he had ever heard. "Sunkist oranges are wonderful! I got one when I had measles, and I always used to get them on my birthday." He sniffed at a big orange he was holding. "Whenever I smell an orange I think of my birthday."

But Nils didn't really want to think about his birthday too much. It was coming soon, but it would not be the same thing without Mother and Father and Bix. Of course, it was fine and important to be ten years old.

Nils found that these oranges tasted even better than he remembered they had in Denmark. Mr. Mitchell said that was because here they were tree-ripened; but Denmark was so far away that they had to be shipped green, and ripen on the way.

He and Mrs. Mitchell took Nils through flag-decorated streets to a big Exhibition Hall where there was an orange show going on. In front of the building grew millions of California poppies and, inside, Nils saw a most beautiful lady with a crown on, who was the Orange Queen. Nils saw so many oranges he dreamed of them that night. But before he went to bed he wrote a letter to Mother, because in the morning he was to get the bus and go up in the mountains to Twin Peaks where Uncle Piper lived.

San Bernardino

Dear Mother and Bix,

I am on my way to Uncle Piper at Twin Peaks. Now you have to come soon because I am so lonesome and I need you and Father so much.

Em and Dwi and Aunt Bea and Lena were my good friends and I miss them very much. Mr. Mitchell is nice but I don't really know him. And I hardly remember Uncle Piper at all—only that he taught me to whittle with a knife once. I don't like going to Twin Peaks really—I just don't like mountains. I am an island boy. Even down here the only water I have seen was in small fountains on the grass. They pipe it underneath, and the little springs come up to water the grass.

I have seen real orange trees with oranges on them —oranges I could pick and eat. I have seen eucalyptus trees and palms and pepper trees—really there is more than I can tell you in a letter. You come over here and you will hear all about it.

When you come, maybe we can get an island again. Bea says there are islands in Maine and I will ask Father about them when I see him. I do hope I will see him soon; that is the reason I left the Rancho Arroyo.

Dear Mother and Bix, I am longing very much to see you both.

Nils

Address:
Thor Piper, Twin Peaks, California

The mountain bus next morning was not at all like a Greyhound. It was a short, strong-looking car rather like a bear. Nils got the seat next to the driver, and his suitcases and a big wooden crate of oranges from Mr. Mitchell went in back. His trunk was on top. The only other passenger got out before the bus reached the mountains, so when they began to climb, Nils was alone with the driver.

For three hours the bus went on, higher and higher. The road was so narrow that two cars could barely pass. In the middle was a yellow line to show where each car had to go. The driver kept pointing out things to Nils

and saying, "Isn't that a fine view?" But Nils was so afraid the driver couldn't watch the view and the road too that he could not really enjoy it. Looking out and down made him feel rather sick in his stomach.

Whish! Around a curve. And whish! around another curve. A high wall on one side and a deep chasm down on the other, and a yellow line in the middle. Then the car stalled and Nils got so scared it would roll back down the mountain that his hands were wet.

The driver got out and pulled up the hood. With its mouth open like that, the bus looked as unhappy as a man at the dentist's. The driver gave it a new spark plug, and off they went again, but the man kept muttering about the kind of company that wouldn't give them decent cars for these hard roads. Nils got still more scared. The bus coughed, and he filled his chest and stomach full of air, trying to help it along. It didn't help.

Over another mountain they went, past a town called Crestline, then over Blue Jay Point to Twin Peaks on still another mountain. Whish! around one curve after another. Nils had never seen such mountains, even in New Mexico; these were steeper and craggier with deeper chasms to fall into if the bus should slip. It grew colder, and they got up into the snow. Nils put on his big coat, and the car steamed like smoke. The road was icy and slippery.

They came at last to a post office in a big pine forest. The driver said, "I can't take you any farther." And he threw Nils' suitcases and oranges and trunk off into the snow.

Nils didn't even know where the house was that he was going to, but when he went to the post office to ask, he got a letter from Uncle Piper. It just said, "I will not be home until late. Here is the key to the kitchen door. It is the last house on the hill. You are to sleep in the studio."

Nils asked the postmaster what he should do with all his luggage out there in the snow. But the postmaster said he couldn't leave his office and it was four miles to Mr. Piper's place. Nils had better ask Frenchy at the store.

At the store, Frenchy was busy. There were lumberjacks sitting on high stools at a counter and drinking coffee. They were all surprised to see a boy with a tanned face and hair so light it was like tow. Where had he come from? Where was he going? Where were his mother and father? How old was he? Nils answered them all politely and then asked Frenchy what he should do. Frenchy said he would get his son.

By the time Frenchy came back with his son, Nils had decided he had better buy some food if Uncle Piper was away. He had some of the money Father had sent him for his trip. Feeling very practical, he began to buy things: a dozen eggs, a box of sugar, a box of matches, a big package of chocolate, a can of coffee for Uncle Piper to have when he came back, a can of condensed milk and a box of the pancake flour that had the smiling colored lady on it. Then he added bacon, so he could have pancakes with bacon. He could not think of anything else.

"What about bread and butter?" Frenchy's son asked.

Nils wondered how he could have forgotten. He bought the bread and butter and a slab of yellow cheese. Then he paid for everything, and it all went into a brown paper sack as big as his little sister Bix. He wouldn't die of starvation for a few days, but he did not have so much money left in his pocket.

In the end both Frenchy and his son went in the car to take Nils up to Uncle Piper's house. It was a good thing they did, too, because they had a lot of trouble getting up the hillside, which seemed to go straight up in the air. They had to put chains on the tires and use a shovel to dig the car out of the snow several times.

It was the last house, all right, a log house on the edge of the precipice. The grounds seemed to be filled up with logs and planks and pots and pans. The trees were so tall they nearly touched the sky, and Nils got a stomach ache when he looked down, far down to the valley.

Nils gave Frenchy the key to open the padlock on the door, and all his suitcases and his trunk and box of oranges were thrown into the kitchen. There wasn't any room left. There were black pots and pans on the wall, bottles and cans everywhere, and among them enormous wood sculptures. A black pipe went up and across the room in a funny, twisty way, and out through the wall. It rose from a big rusty stove that was stone cold.

There was a wooden staircase with a crooked curtain hanging on nails. A table held more wood sculptures and a lot of tools, so Nils wasn't sure whether this was a kitchen or a studio. The letter said he was to sleep in the studio, but he didn't see any bed either under the staircase or under the table. Uncle Piper certainly had a funny way of arranging his house, and it looked as if nobody had lived there for a month.

Frenchy and his son were looking as surprised as Nils when he paid them a dollar for bringing him up to this peculiar house. They rumbled off down through the snowy forest with a clatter of chains, and Nils was alone on a mountaintop in that funny barracks.

The sun came out and Nils went outside. It was certainly beautiful! There were more very high mountains far away, and Nils wondered if that was where his father was now. A lot of blue jays made a great racket among the trees. There were some big rocks, round and as tall as Nils, behind the house, and back of them was the deep, deep valley. There was already dark blue shadow down there, and Nils could see lights twinkling in houses in some little town. Up on the mountains on the other side of the canyon, the nearly setting sun was very red.

Nils had to hurry to make himself a meal before dark. He brought in pine cones and branches and stuffed them into the cold stove. He cooked eggs and bacon and a pan of good hot chocolate. He was soon warm and fed, but it was getting dark and he still had to find his bed. He hurried up the staircase behind the curtain to find two more studios, one with a painting on an easel, the other with a typewriter and a lot of papers everywhere, on the chairs as well as the table. Uncle Piper must be a very busy man, or else three or four people worked here. No bed, though.

Nils went downstairs again and found another door. That led to a big, big studio with windows on three sides —about five windows on each wall. There was a big table with a tablecloth, and it was all set for him, with plates and dates and figs and bread and butter—and a letter.

"Welcome, Nils," the letter said. "Eat, and here is your bed in the studio. Light the fire."

It was very nice of Uncle Piper to fix everything for him. He had even spelled out Nils' name in green leaves on the table. The fireplace was as big as a whole house, with logs and whole trees in it; Nils did not dare set fire to all that. And he did not feel like sleeping in that enormous room with all those windows, and all the big statues of marble and wood.

He took blankets and went upstairs to the room with the painting, which was of a sunset over a lot of clouds. There was a sort of couch there on three logs. In this house there were logs everywhere, as if Uncle Piper cut down another tree every time he needed a piece of wood.

It grew so dark that Nils could not see anything more. He rolled himself up in blankets, but it was quite a long time before he could go to sleep.

12. Uncle Piper

Nils was wakened in the night by an awful noise! He
was so frightened his hair stood on end. The door downstairs was forced open with such a racket that the whole

house shook. A dog was barking—*bow-wow-wow!* Then a voice, "Hello, Nils, where are you?"

Nils went down. There was Uncle Piper, lighting a candle that Nils hadn't seen. "Keep quiet, Petersen!" Uncle Piper told his dog. "Why are you in bed so early, Nils?"

"It was so dark and cold," Nils said.

"Why didn't you build a fire?"

"It was too big," said Nils.

"Too big? Can a fire be too big in this cold?" Uncle Piper dumped down a lot of cases of canned food and about twenty loaves of bread and went in to the studio to put a match to the kindling under the log in the fireplace. Whee! The big fir tree burned like powder. Soon there was a nice warm place around the big granite fireplace.

"Now eat, and we will talk," Uncle Piper said.

Nils ate again, and Uncle Piper pulled the bed over to the fire. Then they both sat on it and talked.

"Your Daddy won't be able to get over from Bear Mountain in this snow," Uncle Piper told Nils, "but you are all right here, aren't you?"

"Yes," said Nils, feeling all right now that Uncle Piper had come.

Uncle Piper was a funny-looking fellow, even odder than Nils had remembered him. He had a little red nose and three-cornered eyes and no eyebrows at all. He had long, thin yellow hair, and he was dressed in ski trousers and an orange sweater; he had a purple neckerchief and he wore wooden shoes. Petersen lay in his lap, a little brown and white spotted fox terrier with intelligent eyes. At a high yapping bark outside, Petersen lifted one ear and growled.

"What's that?" asked Nils.

"That's just the coyotes," Uncle Piper said.

"Oh, there were coyotes at Pojoaque, too. There aren't any wolves here, are there, Uncle Piper?"

"Oh, yes, sure, I've seen them. Once after a fire up in the Sierra Nevada Mountains the wolves came down here. You can meet bears, too, on the way to the post office. And what do you think—one night I went down under the house to get some wood and a mountain lion flew out!"

Nils wasn't feeling quite so all right any more. It was a good thing Uncle Piper had come home. Uncle Piper wasn't afraid of any of those animals, though. He thought they were very interesting, and he told Nils about rattle-snakes and black widow spiders and scorpions. Even the

ground squirrels were dangerous, he said, and people down in the valley were dying from a disease they caught from the ground squirrels.

Why, Nils had seen a ground squirrel that very day

when he was gathering pine cones! He wondered if he would ever get down off this mountain alive. He felt as stiff as a block of ice, and he kept looking through the dark windows for a mountain lion, and peering at the logs to see if there were any black widow spiders or scorpions.

"Don't you want to sleep down here by the fire?" Uncle Piper asked.

Nils looked at all those windows again. "No, thank you, Uncle Piper. May I sleep upstairs, please?"

"Sure, if you like that better," said Uncle Piper, rather surprised.

The sun was rising like a big fireworks display over the Bear Mountains when Uncle Piper called Nils.

"Five o'clock, Nils! Get up! Out to get some pine cones!"

Five o'clock was terribly early for a boy as tired as Nils was, but he scrambled into his clothes and tumbled downstairs.

"Here is a sack for the cones," Uncle Piper said. "Then you can chop a little wood. By then you will be warm and your breakfast will be ready."

Nils went out under the pine trees, where there were lots of cones. Suddenly he remembered the rattlesnakes. And the black widow spiders. And the scorpions. And the ground squirrels with the disease. He scurried back indoors.

"The sack is only half full!" Uncle Piper said. "Out again, my friend!"

The house already smelled of bacon and coffee, but Nils had to go out. When he had filled the cone sack he had to go back to chop wood—such big pieces of wood he could not get the ax through them! Everything in America was bigger than it was anywhere else. He had to go back and admit to Uncle Piper that he could not chop the wood.

"I'll show you how!" Uncle Piper laughed. He grabbed a bigger ax from the corner of the kitchen. He set a big log on end. "Now watch!"

Uncle Piper took the ax between his legs; he swung it up in the air over his head, bent his body in a bow, and —smack! The log was in two pieces from top to bottom.

Uncle Piper finished the wood-chopping that morning, and they went in to breakfast. But just as they sat down Uncle Piper started up again, grabbed his rifle, and shot from the doorway—*bang-bang!* This was a shock to Nils.

"A ground squirrel," said Uncle Piper calmly. "We'll burn it after breakfast. Now let's eat."

Several days passed, and Nils was kept busy all the time. He swept the house, washed the dishes, cleaned out ashes, chopped wood, peeled potatoes. Uncle Piper was busy too, tapping away on the typewriter.

"I am glad to have you here, Nils," he said. "You are a real help. Can you hurry down to the post office for me? I haven't time to go."

Nils went the four miles to the post office. On the way he thought he saw a bear. And he knew he saw an owl and two eagles. He found a stone that looked as if it had gold all over it. He saw a lot of squirrels but only one ground squirrel. He found a beautiful yellow butterfly, but it was frozen dead.

The sun was shining and the snow had gone. The trees were enormous. They looked as if two or three little trees were growing on top of them. Nils was sure that those small trees on top of the great big ones were as large as the firs at home in Denmark.

Petersen was with Nils. He chased every squirrel, jumping over dead logs like a deer. But he was a good dog and always came back when Nils whistled for him.

At the post office there was a letter and a newspaper for Uncle Piper, but nothing for Nils.

When Nils came home he asked Uncle Piper why there were so many dead trees on top of the mountain, and some ruins of houses up there, too. "Oh, that was a forest fire," Uncle Piper said. "It jumped from one mountain to the next and burned three houses and all the forest down to Arrowhead on that side. It burned down the big Arrowhead Hotel, too."

"Can the animals save themselves when there's a fire?" Nils asked.

"Most of the time. They run in big packs, even enemies like wolves and deer, side by side. If they have little ones they don't leave them, though. Sometimes people can't even get down because the fire shuts off the roads."

Nils didn't feel like asking any more questions. But his imagination did not stop working.

"Nils, do you know how to make orange marmalade?" Uncle Piper asked.

Nils didn't.

"Well, we have to use up all those oranges you brought. You can read, can't you?—and there's a cookbook here someplace." Uncle Nils had been reading his letter. "You can make marmalade while I'm away. You wouldn't be afraid to stay here alone with Petersen for a night, would you?"

"No, I—I don't think so. Are you going away, Uncle Piper?"

"Yes, I have to go down to Long Beach. There's a lady wants to see me about making a woodcut for her. I'll take the bus at the post office at four o'clock and come back tomorrow—if I catch the bus. Maybe Mrs. Balfour will drive me back. You cook up all those oranges and lemons and grapefruit today. Let them stand overnight, and then cook them up again tomorrow with all the sugar we have. The glasses are in that closet—they'll have to be washed. You know where the dog food is."

All the time Uncle Piper was giving his orders he was getting shaved and putting on a white shirt and black trousers and a black velvet jacket. When he put on a black beret he looked like a French artist, except that his face was not at all French. Nils was surprised that he could look so nice, and that even his shoes were cleaned.

"Now, remember, Nils, when the sun comes out—if it does tomorrow—you take the slices of bread out of all the packages and dry them in the sun, first on one side, then on the other. Otherwise the whole business will mold. Then you can store them in these two drawers. Well, good-by now, Nils. Take good care of the house."

Uncle Piper was gone. Petersen went with him and did not come back. All afternoon Nils peeled and sliced fruit and burned pine cones to cook it. He was sticky up to his elbows from the juice and the pitch from the cones.

Nils was dreadfully tired when he got through with the marmalade for that day. Uncle Piper had no mirror, so he did not know how dirty he was. And he was too tired to cook himself dinner, so he ate bread and honey and wiped his fingers on the back of his trousers. He went outside to look at the mountains and the valley.

But where *was* the valley? There were only clouds. Nils could look down at the tops of clouds that covered all the towns down there. They looked like a big ocean with an island far off on the other side where the top of Bear Mountain stuck up through the fog.

The clouds were rising. They filled the canyon toward the Sierra Nevada Mountains; they drifted in among all the firs and pines and cedars. Suddenly it looked as if two winds from different directions were fighting with the clouds. They boiled up into the air. Nils had never seen such a fight before. Then—*bang!*—came the thunder, louder than Nils had ever heard it in his life.

Nils scurried back into the house, chased by the clouds, which swirled all round the house now. From the windows he couldn't see even the closest trees. It was dark

among the clouds, except when lightning cut through them with blinding flashes. Lightning could start a forest fire. And Nils was up here on the mountaintop all alone!

It started to rain. It rained in through the walls, under the door, around the windows. Nils used every rag he could find to try to sop it up, but it was a losing battle.

The wind blew; thunderclaps banged; the whole house rocked. *Bang!* Another thunderclap, and it seemed as if the whole house had fallen in on itself. Nils went green in the face and had to sit down because his legs wouldn't hold him up.

In a lull between thunderclaps he heard a crying voice from under the kitchen staircase. It must be a mountain lion! He latched the door and ran upstairs to his bed. It was wet up there too, and the whole house seemed to be swinging. He remembered that Uncle Piper had told him that the roof was not fastened on and the house was only built on some stones.

Nils crept into bed with his clothes on and covered his ears with the blanket so he could not hear. But he could not stop hearing. Whenever the thunder stopped, he could hear the mountain lion crying under the kitchen. If that lion got in, what on earth was he to do?

"*Wooow! Oooo! Wuuuw!*"

Could a mountain lion really cry like that? Nils was listening for it now. And between thunder crashes he heard it again.

"Petersen!" Nils yelled. "Oh, Petersen, where are you?" He rushed down the stairs. "Petersen, where are you?"

"*Mmmmmoooo! Wooow!*" Petersen didn't sound like

a mountain lion howling now, but like a lonely little dog wanting to come in.

Right against the wall under the staircase Nils discovered a loose board. There was a handle to pull it up by. In came Petersen in a big rush, jumping and licking at Nils. He was used to coming in by that hole, and he must have thought Nils a very stupid boy to take so long to let him in.

The little terrier was as wet as a drowned mouse, but he was happy and so was Nils. They both got into bed with the covers over their heads. Hugging Petersen in his arms, Nils listened to the thunderstorm raging and fighting like wild animals round the mountain.

The elements fought all night, but Petersen and Nils went to sleep. The house shook and waggled, but only a little studio building out on the mountainside went down into the valley with an awful *ratabang*. It was a good thing Nils was asleep then or he would have died of fright.

13. Happy Birthday

In the morning the wind was not so angry. The sheets of paper that Uncle Piper had fastened to the rafter with thumbtacks were still flapping like the sails of a full-rigged schooner, but the house was not rocking now.

Nils got up to see the sun shining on a fairy-tale winter landscape. Outside the window was a pine tree, and every one of its needles was covered with a long prickle of ice. The rain had frozen and changed it into a gigantic ice flower. Every needle shone with rainbow colors when the sun touched it, and it was so bright that Nils had to blink.

Nils himself was not so beautiful, but he could not see how he looked. His nose was red. His face was still greenish. His white hair stuck out in every direction. His clothes were rumpled and covered with white dog hairs. If there had been a mirror, how Nils would have laughed at himself! But Uncle Piper did not want a mirror. "I am so ugly it would hurt my sense of beauty to look into it," he always said.

Nils peeped out of the door. It was bitter cold, but a lot of pine cones had fallen. He didn't think there could be rattlesnakes or scorpions or black widow spiders left after that storm, but he borrowed Uncle Piper's wooden shoes to be safe, and put on mittens. He could hardly believe his eyes when he saw that the little studio was gone completely!

Nils brought in cones. He made oatmeal and chocolate and heated the bread on the stove.

The sun vanished again. It rained and rained, and the wind came back. It was dark and nasty by eleven o'clock, when Uncle Piper had said he ought to be back.

Nils waited and waited. Uncle Piper didn't come. Twelve o'clock—one—two. Nils stood at the window for three hours.

At four o'clock, Nils knew, the bus ought to go down

to San Bernardino. He would *not* stay here any longer—
not through another stormy night all alone. He packed
his little suitcase as Uncle Piper had done, putting in his
toothbrush and pajamas. He closed Petersen into the
kitchen with food and water. He wrote a note and stuck
it on the door with a thumbtack. "I have gone to Mr.
Mitchell's in San Bernardino. The key is in the secret
place." Then he added, in case Uncle Piper should forget his secret place, "Under the table in the sun porch."

And he left the mountaintop, the marmalade, nice
Petersen, and his trunks. He didn't care right then.

He ran along the road, seeing nothing on either side this time. Everything was lost in fog. There might be another thunderstorm. There might be a forest fire. The house might blow over the edge of the mountain as the little studio had done. The mountain lion might come, or the squirrels give him that disease.

Nils got to the post office, dirty and freezing. The postmaster's wife was startled at the sight of him. "I have to go down to San Bernardino on the four-o'clock bus," he told her.

"But there is no mail bus today, Nils. We'll have to telephone for a car."

"Will that be awfully expensive?" Nils asked. He had five dollars and eighty cents left of the money Father had sent him.

"Usually it is five dollars, Nils. But you know the mail bus has to go if we have a passenger. So they will have to send a car, and it will cost a dollar and a quarter."

She telephoned, and a taxicab came from the nearest town. It had a lady chauffeur who picked up Nils' suitcase and nodded at him encouragingly. "Now don't you be afraid even if it is slippery today," she said. "I'll get you there safe and sound. Just don't bother your head about all the accidents that happen on this mountain road. It is only when people drive on the wrong side of that line in the middle of the road that there is real danger."

Nils had not heard about the accidents before, so his eyes fairly popped out of his head, watching to see that she was staying on the right side of the line. It was dark as night, although it was only half past four, and the lady turned her fog lights on. They went round big rocks and wound in and out. Nils could not see the precipice now, but he knew it was there! Soon he couldn't even see the line in the middle of the road. He didn't think the lady could either!

Whizzing round, first to the left, then to the right, the lady told him all about all the accidents that had happened on the road. Nils was stiff with terror. "This fog isn't going to lift until tomorrow or the day after," the lady said. Nils didn't think he would ever reach San Bernardino alive.

Suddenly—it was like a miracle—they came out of the fog, as if they had driven right through a wall into the sun! It was sunset over the San Bernardino Valley, the light all golden between red clouds. He could see the towns again—Redlands, Pomona, Riverside—looking small in the distance. He could even—the greatest miracle of all—see the coast and the houses of Long Beach beside the ocean!

The dark mountains had disappeared in the clouds above, and Nils did not want to see them again. The lady pulled up on a flat turnout so Nils could look at the view. There were some other cars pulled up there too.

And, can you believe it, Nils' father was in one of them!

He was on his way up to see Nils at Twin Peaks. He had seen the car come out of the clouds, and he had stopped to ask how the road was. Nils had never been so excited in his whole life.

Father paid the lady driver and thanked her, and got Nils into his own car. "Boy, how you look!" he said.

Nils put his arms round Father's neck, and he told him about the storm and the wild animals and the poisonous squirrels and the disease everywhere, and scorpions and black widow spiders, and how Uncle Piper had gone away.

"It's all nonsense!" Father said. "I knew Piper was a little peculiar, but I didn't think he would scare the wits out of a young man like you."

"Well, it's all right now that you are here!" Nils said. "Everything is fine."

"Well, promise me never to look like this again, Nils.

Do you know what you look like? A child who doesn't have any mother or father and hasn't had anything to eat."

"There isn't any mirror at Twin Peaks," Nils excused himself.

"I can imagine," Father said. "Why are your arms so dirty?"

"Oh, that's the marmalade and the stove and pine cones. I was making marmalade all day yesterday out of Mr. Mitchell's oranges."

"Why did you do a thing like that, Nils?"

"Uncle Piper told me to do it. He was going away, you see."

Father was angry as he thought about Nils being up on the mountain all alone in that terrible storm. But now they would just go on up and get Nils' luggage and then drive back down. They would go to Long Beach.

"Careful!" Nils whispered as Father rounded a bend. "A car fell two hundred feet down the hill here, and hung in a pine tree."

"Who told you that?" asked Father.

"The lady who drove me down. She told me about a lot of other accidents too."

At Uncle Piper's house, Father got Nils' trunk and the other suitcases and he wrote Uncle Piper a letter. By the time they left, Nils was a nice clean boy again. He would have liked to take Petersen along, but Father said they could not do that. Petersen was Uncle Piper's dog and his only friend when he lived up there alone.

Father drove slowly back down the dark, foggy mountain road, on the right side of the line. Nils was not at all frightened now. They came out of the fog into the clear night. They could count seven towns in the valley with lights like clusters of pepper berries.

"Can you see the lights far away over there by the ocean?" Father asked. "That is Long Beach. You and I are going there and stay at the big hotel called the Long Beach Casino."

"Golly!" said Nils. "Isn't that terribly expensive?"

"I guess we'll manage it." Father smiled. "It is your birthday gift."

Birthday gift! Why, tomorrow was Nils' birthday and he had been so upset he had forgotten all about it. And Father said he had a birthday letter from Mother for Nils too.

By the time they got to the Casino, Nils was too sleepy to be overawed by the big hotel. But the next day he could really appreciate it. He and Father went swimming. He had the birthday letter from Mother and Bix. Father had got them a front room on the ocean, and he said they were going to stay here for two weeks.

So Nils' tenth birthday party lasted for two whole

weeks. Every morning they had an icy cold swim and then went in to a big breakfast with waffles and honey and orange juice and oatmeal and cream. They went for long drives along the shore. They even went on a fishing trip to Santa Monica, in a motorboat that took them out to a mother ship where there were lots of people with fishing poles. They went to the movies, and at night they sat up on the roof terrace of the hotel to watch the moon on the water.

The end of this birthday celebration was the best of all. A letter from Mother was forwarded to Father. Mother was going to get her entry permit at last, and in a few weeks more she would be with them!

"The letter was mailed the nineteenth of April," Father said, "and today is the twenty-second. Four days for an air letter—that is not bad."

It seemed wonderful to Nils.

"Where are we going to live?" Nils asked. "You know, Father, there is a place called Maine—clear over on the other side of America—where they have a lot of islands. Do you suppose—"

Father did suppose. He had been thinking of getting a new home for his family in Maine. In fact, he had told

Bea about that in a letter to her, and that was why Bea had talked to Nils about Maine.

Nils thought it was very wonderful how things worked out.

14. Happy Ending

One day a great white ship sailed into New York harbor and went slowly up the river to her pier. It was the *Gripsholm.*

Against the ship's rail, Mother was holding Bix high in her arms. Bix was waving both chubby hands. Beside Father on the pier, Nils danced with joy, capering until everybody was laughing at him and with him.

Mother and Bix came down a covered gangway, and then what hugging and kissing there was! Under a big letter H, which hung from the ceiling, they stood among suitcases and trunks, and the long months of waiting melted away like fog when the sun comes out.

It was a very happy little family that drove in Father's car to their new home in Maine.

"I've been up here once already with Father," Nils told Mother. "Our place is right on the edge of the sea. There are lots of pretty islands that we can row out to for picnics. The house is dear, too. We only have to make some new doors and windows and paint the outside and clear the weeds out of the garden. And put new wallpaper inside. You will like it."

"Now, Nils, don't scare your mother," Father said with a laugh. Then he told Mother, "Don't be afraid, it isn't so bad. It is really a delightful old farm. And you won't have to stay there right away. We are going to Little Ponds to stay with some good friends in their beautiful white house until I have the farm completely fixed up for you. And all the furniture you shipped will be in the rooms when you move in."

The little family looked forward with joy to the farm. It might be only walls and a roof now, but it would not stay that way long. And they were all together again— that was the really important thing!